A BROOKHAVEN PARANORMAL COZY MYSTERY
BOOK 4

HIGH HOPES

S.E. BIGLOW

If you enjoy this work, please consider leaving a review.

For information contact; www.sarah-biglow.com

Edited by Under Wraps Publishing

Cover Design by: Deranged Doctor Design

Print ISBN: 978-1-955988-31-5

Published by S.E. Biglow: September 2023

10 9 8 7 6 5 4 3 2 1

1

———

Spring came to Brookhaven in subtle ways. Newly grown shoots of grass and flowers began to unfurl against the chilly temperatures and gusting winds. My magic wanted to be outside helping the flora along, but my body was far happier curled up beneath a blanket in the living room of Tania's B&B with a hot mug of coffee. At present, I sat in the kitchen, mentally fortifying myself for the trip to work. I watched bare branches with the tiniest hints of new leaves at their tips, flailing helplessly in the gales of wind that whistled through the backyard. If I didn't know any better, I'd expect a tornado to come rampaging through the small town and lift the house off its foundation with the howling gusts.

"You look miserable," commented Sam, the B&B's resident ghost, when I turned back to my coffee.

I took a moment to study his appearance. Most days, Sam looked like he was about to walk a runway, decked out in flashy eye make-up and sequined outfits. Today, he sported a more muted deep purple velvet jacket and sleek black pants. In the back of my mind, I wondered if the strange dichotomy of springtime in New England had dampened his mood, too.

"Not miserable," I corrected, gesturing to the outdoors with a flourish. "Just not happy to be venturing out in this."

"You do have the car," he pointed out.

Tania, the proprietor of the B&B and my mentor on all things magical, had lent me use of her VW Bug since I'd moved in seven months ago. Even still, I wasn't confident in my ability to keep the car on the road. "With my luck, I'd wind up getting blown away."

"Just admit you need a day off," he chided. "I'm sure Sage would give you a sick day."

Sage owned the town's marijuana dispensary, High Time, and had been gracious enough to hire me after I helped root out a thief in its ranks. I felt bad bailing on her and the business, even if a day off sounded lovely. "... I've got the weekend off," I finally said and downed the rest of my coffee for fortification.

Sam offered a silent shrug as I stepped around him to rinse out the mug and set it on the drain board. I looked around the kitchen—it was unusually quiet—and turned back to Sam. Before I'd arrived, Tania's business was struggling to stay afloat. Things had picked up a little since I'd moved to Brookhaven and became a resident at her B&B, not that I counted myself as the reason. Though we'd still gone a decent stretch through the winter without many visitors. "I thought Tania said we'd have some new guests coming in this week."

"She's out shopping. Apparently, one of the guests has some kind of food allergy or something. She was even panicking for hours before you got up ... worried that they wouldn't have anything to eat."

I didn't bother asking how long she'd been up before me, considering I'd climbed out of bed at six thirty. "Well, tell her I'll be back late. I've got dinner with Maggie tonight."

Sam gave a graceful spin and made a kissy face at me. "Sod off," I said with a laugh before donning a coat and gripping the car keys in my hand.

"Let me live vicariously through you," he said with a pout.

Maggie, the town's healer, and I had officially been a couple for the last few months. Technically our first date was attending the biggest wedding in town last November. At least until the groom had turned up dead. Murder tended to put a damper on romance. But we'd vowed to go on a proper, murder-free date in the New Year. Three months since then and things were going better than I could have hoped.

I wanted to tell Sam to find someone else's life to enjoy, but I didn't have the heart. He was just being cheeky. I couldn't imagine being a ghost, existing just on the outside of so many things. Then again, I'd never met any other ghosts and Sam was rather private about both his time among the living and his afterlife. We traded jabs now and again. Yet, I still didn't feel comfortable asking about the subject of his death or what unfinished business might be keeping him tethered here.

The thought of seeing Maggie this evening buoyed my spirits enough that I even avoided cursing the weather gods as the wind blew me sideways into the hood of Tania's Bug. I caught my balance enough to climb in, the wind slamming the door on me. Making the brief trip down Main Street to High Time much less treacherous than I'd envisioned in my head. And by the time I got inside, the gusts had died down.

I passed through the kitchen and into the employee locker rom. I stowed my coat and situated my ID, ready to head into the growth chamber to tend to the plants when Sage appeared. Her aqua-colored hair shone brighter in the overhead lighting. She must have just redone it. It appeared to match the vibrancy of her expression when she spotted me.

"Morning, Darcy," she greeted. "I was hoping to catch you before your shift started."

A lump formed in my throat. Impromptu conversations were not my favorite thing. I was still one of the newest employees on the roster and the only one that I knew of on a work visa. "Uh, sure ... morning. Is everything okay?"

"Everything's fine. I just wanted to let you know that I'm getting a shipment in of some new strains I wanted to try. I think they're going to be really good for business."

Relief washed over me, sending waves of warmth cascading through my body. "Oh, okay. I'll get some bays ready for transplanting then."

"Great. Thanks. I'll let you know when they arrive."

Stepping into the temperature-controlled growth chamber, I let out a sigh. I wasn't one to partake in the products we sold here, but I did find being around the plants soothing. Exposing myself to them nearly every day had given me the chance to hone my powers. When I'd first arrived in town, I could barely control my powers and wasn't even sure I wanted them. Now, I couldn't imagine my life without having that constant, if subtle connection to every living thing that grew around me.

So much of my hesitation to embrace my magic stemmed from my family. When I'd told my parents about how I thought I could hear plants in my head, trying to garner my attention to nurture them, they'd scoffed at me. My mum had insisted I was just trying to get attention. She and my dad made it perfectly clear they didn't believe me.

Since moving to Brookhaven, I'd learned that magic was hereditary. It had to come from one side of my family line, even if they didn't want to acknowledge it. In some ways this only left me with more questions that I doubted would ever be answered. I couldn't talk to either of them about where these powers came from. Dad's parents were both long dead and both of my parents were only children with no siblings. So, it wasn't like I had aunts or cousins to ask. But my Nan was still around and thankfully she hadn't called me crazy when she'd heard what I'd been dealing with.

As I sat surrounded by marijuana seedlings in various stages of growth, I couldn't help picturing my Nan in her showy pink cardigan and oversized earrings. I hadn't talked to her much since moving to the States and I missed her. If Tania were around, she'd probably tell me she could feel the longing that had crept into my chest, making it that little bit harder to breathe. But I didn't need an empath to know I'd been cutting myself off from the one person who might actually accept me and my magic for no good reason. I resolved to reach out on my lunch break. Today was as good a time as any to get in touch.

By the time my phone read 12:20, the new plants Sage had warned about arrived. I situated them in separate bays offset from the existing crop of plants and purposely set them up with their own dedicated growth lights.

"Right you lot, let's see what makes you so special," I whispered.

I dug my fingers into the soil, making sure I

made contact with the plants' stems. I could feel tiny pulses of energy moving through them as they took notice of my power. I closed my eyes, waiting for them to reveal what they might one day become. That was how my magic had first presented itself to me. Every flower I passed whispered in my head what it could one day be. I'd been afraid of that potential for so long. Not now though. In fact, I was convinced if Tania hadn't filled the B&B with plants for me to nurture in the winter months, I'd have gone mad from the silence.

The tiny seedlings in my hands trembled. I could see them in my mind's eye fully grown. More importantly I could feel what they could do—the pain they could relieve, the anxiety they could curb. The dispensary sold several products aimed at alleviating those conditions, but I could feel the potency in these seedlings. Sage was right; they were going to be great for business.

I pulled my fingertips free and smoothed the soil back into place. Maybe it was the prolonged exposure, or it was just in my head, but as I headed for the locker room to get my coat, a sense of calm washed over me. Any nerves I'd had about reaching out to Nan, for the moment, evaporated. A girl could get used to that.

I walked to Ginny's—the town's only decent diner—and snagged a spot at the counter on the far end. As was to be expected of the owner, Ginny Hayes sat on the center stool along the same counter, holding court. As the town's resident gossip, she had a way of getting people to spill their secrets to her. Like me, she was a witch. She pivoted on her stool to face me, offering a genuine smile and wave. Things had started off rocky between us. Though these days, I was confident she no longer saw me as a nuisance or a disruption to her hometown's equilibrium. I'd even managed to stay on her brother's good side, which was perhaps much more important. I'd had far too many run-ins for my liking with Rick Hayes, Brookhaven's Chief of Police. For some inexplicable reason I seemed to find trouble in the form of dead bodies in this town. At least the last few months had been peaceful.

I ordered and pulled out my phone while I waited, ready to bite the bullet and place the international call to England. I stared at the screen in surprise when I saw an incoming international call from Nan's number. In that moment, I regretted making the decision to attempt reconnection in such a public space. But I hit the green Accept button anyway and held the phone to my ear.

"Hello?"

"Oh, sweet girl, I thought I'd never hear your voice again," Nan said on the other end of the call.

I let out a nervous laugh. "I wasn't sure I'd ever hear your voice either ..." After a beat, I said, "Nan, this is going to sound a bit mental, but I was literally about to call you."

It was Nan's turn to laugh. "I know you were."

"What?"

"You didn't think you were the only one with special gifts, did you? I owe you an apology, Darcy. When you came to me and shared your new abilities, I should have been there to nurture and help guide you. But your mum had always refused to believe in magic, and I let that get in the way."

"So, what, you can see the future?"

"Not entirely, but I do get a sense of things to come."

Part of me was relieved to know I could actually talk to someone in my family about my powers. Tania was wonderful and a good friend, but there was just something special about sharing it with someone whose blood flowed in your veins. Except another part of me couldn't hide the hurt she'd shut me out. "Finding my way was hard."

"I am truly sorry for that, love. I want to make it up to you."

"How? You aren't planning a transatlantic flight, are you?"

When she laughed this time, it was more subdued. "No, love. Not right now, anyway. But I thought you ought to know that we aren't the only ones with gifts in our family. My sister, Pauline, left England when we were barely adults and moved to the States."

A loud buzzing echoed in my ears as my brain fought to make sense of her words. There was the possibility of having family on the same continent as me? Had Nan known I'd settle in Brookhaven because it was closer to family that might accept me?

"Where is she now? Can I talk to her?"

"We exchanged letters for a while. I know that she settled down in New York and got married. Sadly, we lost touch over the years. I only recently discovered that she has a daughter and a grand-daughter of her own."

"Did she reach back out to you?"

"No, I went on one of those ancestry sites and it showed me information about Pauline's family. I can send it to you if you'd like."

"I would really like that." The waiter came by,

setting down a cup of coffee and a sandwich with fries in front of me. I slid him a twenty dollar bill as I munched on a fry. "Why'd Pauline leave, Nan?"

"Let's just say, your parents weren't the only ones hesitant about embracing magic. Truth be told, I was always jealous of Pauline. She was the free spirit, went where the world pulled her. I stayed put, because I knew that's what my parents needed. Something tells me you take after her more than my side of the family."

"I'm sorry you felt like you couldn't embrace that part of you. I know how painful it is to stifle such an important piece of yourself."

"You've found somewhere to flourish, though, haven't you, my girl?"

I stopped short of telling her that she already knew the answer. Even if her powers had allowed her to see how I was doing, I suspected she would appreciate the report from her granddaughter even more. "I have. I've got a job that I like and friends who accept me. And I'm actually seeing someone."

"Oh, that's wonderful."

"I am really glad you called, Nan," I said as my phone alarm buzzed. I only had fifteen minutes left on my lunch break. "I hate to cut this short, but I've got to get back to work soon."

"Don't let me keep you dear."

"I promise I won't be a stranger."

"That makes me very happy, love." The line went quiet and then Nan added, "I've sent you the information I found on Pauline's family to your email. Whatever you choose to do with it, I know will be the right decision for you."

2

____

By the end of my shift, I was crawling out of my skin to see Maggie and share the information Nan had forwarded to me. Waiting until I finished work to check my email had nearly driven me mad. By the time I clocked out and settled in behind the wheel of the VW Bug, I'd concocted multiple potential scenarios for my stateside relatives. In some, they were a wild bunch of magic-using hippies. While in others, they'd retained their posh British attitudes, but not their accents having assimilated to the local cadence. Any one of them panning out would make me unbelievably happy.

I pulled into one of the few spots in front of Brookhaven's only Italian restaurant, Piazza di Pizza and checked my reflection in the rearview mirror.

My hair had frizzed a bit in the humidity of the growth chamber. I did my best to smooth it down, not that Maggie would mind. Part of me wished I had time to go back to the B&B and change out of my work uniform though.

I walked into the restaurant and took a look around. The place boasted only a dozen four-seater tables and I found Maggie waiting at one situated near the back. The electric candle at the center of the table flickered rhythmically and I was grateful that she'd picked a table not directly beneath the overhead speaker. At least we wouldn't have to yell at each other to be heard.

"I'm not late, am I?" I said, checking the time on my phone.

Maggie stood and offered me a hug and quick kiss on the lips. "No, you're right on time. I finished up early at the clinic today." She still sported her scrubs, which made me feel less self-conscious of my own attire.

She gestured for me to sit down. She was one of the people I felt the most comfortable being around, and yet I still found myself battling nerves. I hadn't had extensive past relationships, so part of me was afraid I'd manage to ruin this. Mercifully, one of the servers came by to take our drink order, returning moments later with two glasses of red wine.

"What should we toast to?" Maggie asked as she held her glass aloft.

"Unexpected connections," I answered. She cocked her head to the side, considering my words.

"To unexpected connections," she agreed and clinked her glass against mine. "Why do I get the feeling there's a story behind those words?"

I took a long sip of wine to fortify myself. "You were unexpected. I honestly never imagined I'd find someone on the other side of the world who under-stood me. Who wanted to know all of me. But here you are. Sometimes, I still can't believe it's real."

"Well, I am more than happy to be the one who could help you open up your heart. Because I happen to think you are pretty special, Darcy."

Heat crept up the nape of my neck at her flattery. "And I also got some news from back in London today."

Maggie set her wine glass down and propped her chin in her right hand. "Tell me."

"It's no secret most of my family thought I was mental when I told them about my magic. It turns out that my Nan has magic, too. She can sort of sense the future." Maybe when I had more time and a chance to do a longer video chat, I'd delve deeper into what she could actually do.

"How'd you find that out?"

"I was planning to call her, but she called me first. She was scared to tell me that she understood what I was going through because she didn't want to lose my mum. But it turns out she has a sister who moved to the States decades back." I could feel my excitement beginning to build.

"So, you could have family here," Maggie replied as the server returned, hovering just out of range. He eyed our unopened menus.

"We need a few more minutes," I told the server and made a show of opening my menu to browse the selection of pastas, sandwiches, and specialty pizzas.

"We should probably figure out what we're ordering," Maggie said, studying her own menu.

The restaurant's business picked up as we decided what to eat. A couple of families settled at the tables closer to the windows. I even spotted my co-worker Thomas dart in for a takeout order. He gave me a quick wave before heading out again. Nothing on the menu drew my attention. When I looked up, Maggie gave me a smile and let out a snort which she attempted to cover with her menu.

"What?" I laid mine down.

"You've just got this look like you want to be anywhere but here right now."

"No, I don't," I protested before hanging my head. "Okay, so maybe I'm a bit distracted." I brushed a few strands of dark curls from my face. "My Nan said that her sister has family here in the States. She sent me everything she got off one of those ancestry websites and I've been waiting all afternoon to open it."

"You have a lot more self-control than I do."

"It's going to sound silly, but I wanted to look at it with you. I can't explain why, but I felt like I needed to share this with you."

"I'm honored." Maggie set aside her menu. "How about we just order a bunch of desserts, go back to my place, and see what she sent you?"

"Yes, please." I waved over the server and downed the rest of my wine. "Can we just see a dessert menu?"

The server looked annoyed at the request, but collected the larger menus from the table. He wound his way through the tables and picked up two half sheet pages offering a listing of their desserts.

I studied the page, zeroing in on the chocolate fudge cake and the chocolate chip cannoli. Where my appetite had been lacking moments earlier, I felt my mouth water as I pictured the sweet pastries. Our server bounced on the balls of his feet, pen at the ready.

We ended up coming away with two orders of fudge cake and half a dozen cannolis. It wasn't a proper meal, but it smelled heavenly. Luckily for us, Maggie's apartment was just one block over. I balanced the takeout bag of desserts while Maggie let us in her building. I trailed her up the two flights of stairs to her second-floor unit.

Ten minutes later, we were curled up on the couch with a plate between us. I savored the richness of the chocolate in the cake. After letting out a soft sigh of satisfaction, I slipped a bit of icing onto the fork.

"This was definitely the right move," I announced, moving the plate so I could rest my head on Maggie's shoulder. "To be honest, going out in public is still a little new for me."

"We've been out together a bunch of times," Maggie said. "But I get it. Being a couple is different than being somewhere as friends."

I craned my neck to look at Maggie. "It's not weird for you, is it? That I feel this way."

She set her fork down and wrapped both of my hands in hers, giving them a firm, reassuring squeeze. "You may not be as far on your journey as I am, but I am patient, and I am not going anywhere. If you would rather just stay here all night, I'm fine with that, too. Because all I care about is spending time with *you*."

I repositioned myself so I could plant a kiss on her lips. "Thank you."

"Now, how about that info your grandmother sent over?" She pulled her laptop off the table and shoved it at me.

Setting the confections aside, I logged into my email to find Nan's message sitting unread at the very top of the screen. My finger wavered over the button to open the correspondence. Once I opened it, the fantasies I'd concocted in my mind over the course of the afternoon would vanish. A part of me feared what I might find instead.

Get it together, Darcy.

I double clicked the message to find an attached PDF file and a brief explanation from Nan. She'd tried her best to compile all the information she'd gathered from the ancestry website on her sister, Pauline. My stomach did a flip as I accessed the attachment.

It was only about ten pages long. The first showed a family tree with Pauline, surname

Dempsey, married to a man called David Finch sixty years ago. I traced the lines down to the next generation—my mother's first cousins—to see they had three children; two sons called Michael and Patrick, and a daughter called Audrey. I studied the sons first, noting they both bore birth and death years. Audrey was the only child of Pauline's left alive now.

Next to Audrey's name, there was a marriage line to a man called Carl Hennessey. They had one child, a daughter called Piper who looked to be only a couple of years younger than me. I scrolled to the next page to find copies of Pauline's marriage license along with documents showing she had become a naturalized citizen at the age of fifty-six. The other pages reflected census data for Pauline and David. He'd been a carpenter by trade when his older children were born. Pauline was listed as a homemaker and in a census a decade later she was listed as a shop owner. There were a couple of photographs included of Pauline and her family, which were a bit yellowed with age. I could see the family resemblance in the shape of our noses and in my great aunt's silhouette. Still, it was clear that my mixed complexion had come from my father's side of the family.

"This is really amazing that your Nan was able to find all of this," Maggie whispered.

"I want to know what happened to Audrey's brothers."

"Keep scrolling. Maybe there's something later on."

The next page covered both Patrick and Michael's fates. They'd both served in the military and were killed in action during Desert Storm. A photograph of Pauline and David—now much older—accepting flags at the burial followed the obituaries for the brothers.

"It must have been so hard losing both of their sons at the same time like that," I said.

"I couldn't even imagine," Maggie agreed. "And for the daughter to be the only child left to carry on the family line. That's a lot of pressure."

The final page revealed Audrey's marriage license and Piper's birth certificate. At least twenty odd years ago, they'd lived in New Hampshire. I wasn't very well acquainted with the geography of the area, but I didn't think it was that far away. I closed the document and sent back a brief thank you to Nan before creating another tab in the browser and opening up Facebook.

"You think you'll be able to find any of them?" Maggie leaned over my shoulder.

"Well, it's worth a shot," I answered with more confidence than I felt.

There couldn't be that many women called Audrey Hennessey living in the Northeastern United States. Besides, I was armed with her maiden name, too. That at least would help me narrow it down. I'd chosen to search for her first. While I suspected Piper had accounts of her own, being able to compare to the information I had from Nan would be easier.

Thankfully, there were only five Audrey Hennesseys on the platform. I could rule out two, because they were under eighteen. That left one located in Palo Alto, California who looked to be a college student. There's one in Ann Arbor, Michigan who appeared to be about the right age, but from the publicly available information it appeared she was single and hadn't been married before. The last one was in Concord, New Hampshire and appeared to be the right age. I clicked on her profile picture and breathed a sigh of relief. It listed her maiden name as Finch. This had to be the right person. I scrolled down through her profile, the information revealed her contacts and found one Piper Hennessey linked at the very top.

Clicking on Piper's picture brought up her profile —what little there was of it for those not on her friends' list. It showed me that she lived in Concord, like her mother. Her profession was listed as Actress.

"This feels like it was meant to be," Maggie said in an encouraging tone.

"Just because I've found her online doesn't mean she'll want to talk to me. Or that she even knows I exist," I reminded her.

"You won't know until you try. It can't hurt to send her a friend request and message explaining who you are."

Swallowing the lump in my throat, I clicked on the button to request we become friends. Then, I opened up a new message and began typing.

Hi Piper, I know I'm writing to you out of the blue, but I've just learned that we're related. My Nan is your grandmother, Pauline's sister. I recently moved to the States and have been feeling a bit disconnected from family. But my Nan passed along some family tree research she'd done, and you were on it. If you're up for it, I'd like for us to get to know each other. Yours, Darcy.

After hitting 'Send' on the message I closed the laptop. There was nothing more to be done tonight. Maggie and I might both be magical, but I was certain it was beyond the bounds of either of our powers to manifest a response on the same night as sending the initial note.

"Nan said that Pauline had magic, too," I said, poking at cake crumbs on the plate between us.

"You're hoping Piper, or her mom have powers, too?" Maggie asked.

"Please don't get me wrong, you and Tania have been amazing with helping me learn to control my magic. I wouldn't trade that for anything. But if either of them do have magic, too, it would just be …. A chance to understand where this power even comes from."

"I understand. Given the way your parents reacted, if I were in your shoes, I'd be hoping they were witches, too. Magic can create an unbelievably strong sisterhood and adding a familial bond makes it even more powerful."

A fresh wave of guilt hit me as I realized I'd been monopolizing the whole evening. "I know this wasn't how you expected tonight to go," I apologized to Maggie.

"I told you already that you didn't need to apologize for anything. I'm just happy we're spending time together." She stroked my hair. "Speaking of spending time together, why don't you stay the night?"

I was about to protest since I hadn't brought anything to change into, but I stopped myself. Maggie was offering the chance to take our relationship farther and I wasn't going to pass up that opportunity.

"I'd like that," I said and leaned in to give her a kiss on the lips.

3

———

 woke the next morning to find the bed beside me empty. I sat up, looking around the familiar surroundings and let out a contented sigh. Even before Maggie and I had become a couple, I'd always felt safe in her home. She'd been so welcoming, even with our first meeting. I did my best to make my hair presentable and even found a spare pair of clothes laid on the foot of the bed for me. I shimmied into the pants and long-sleeved shirt before I made my way out to the combined living room and kitchen area. Maggie stood at the counter, staring intently at the coffee maker.

"Morning," I called.

She spun and gave me a broad smile. "Morning."

"You're in a good mood," I noted as I moved to lean on the breakfast nook. She offered up a one-shoulder shrug, but nudged her laptop closer to me. "I might have peeked this morning."

Confusion clouded my mind for a moment before I remembered I'd sent a message to Piper, my cousin, the night before. "She answered?"

Maggie didn't respond, but she could barely hide her excitement. I grabbed the laptop and studied the screen. I caught the notification that Piper had accepted my friend request. A reply message sat waiting for me in the browser.

> Hi, Darcy! Great to (virtually) meet you. Grammy told me a lot about her family back in England while growing up. I'd always wondered if there were other relatives out there. I'll admit I was never as brave as you to actually go looking. But I'm so glad you decided to reach out. If you're up for meeting, I'd love to grab coffee sometime. Your new cousin, Piper.

"She wants to meet up," I announced, not caring that Maggie likely already knew this information.

"I told you I had a good feeling about this," Maggie replied, setting a fresh cup of coffee down in front of me. As I looked at the words on the screen, my body coursed with energy, and it felt as if I'd already downed five espressos.

"What do I say back?"

"That you'd love to meet up?" she suggested.

I was about to type a response when I noticed Piper's status showed that she was active now. Somehow taking a few sips of the coffee Maggie had prepared calmed my nerves.

> Getting coffee sounds like a good plan. I do have to admit that I don't have the best command of the geography around here. Is there somewhere you'd want to meet that's maybe in between where you are and me here in Brookhaven?

The three tiny dots materialized on the screen almost instantly and by the time I'd taken another sip of coffee, Piper's response flashed on the screen.

> Funny you mention Brookhaven. My troupe is actually putting on a few shows there this weekend and early next week.

My fingers hovered over the keys for a moment as I processed that information. I hadn't heard anything about shows or anyone coming to the town.

"What's wrong?" Maggie prompted as she rounded the island to stand next to me.

"Nothing. She's coming to town already."

"That's quite the coincidence."

My gut tightened as a different scenario came to mind. I had no way of knowing when Piper had accepted my friend request. She could have spent the night looking me up and found out where I lived.

"Or something," I finally muttered.

"If you're feeling nervous, why not suggest you meet at Ginny's. It's public and there are always people around. And if need be, I'm sure you could convince Ginny to help make sure Piper is being truthful."

I glanced toward Maggie. "Are you sure you're not telepathic?"

"If I were in your shoes, I'd be a little skeptical, too. Better to be safe than sorry."

Meeting at Ginny's did put my mind at ease and settled the sloshing in my gut. I turned my attention back to the screen.

That's great. There's a nice café
here in town that makes excellent
coffee. It's called Ginny's on Main
Street. Can't miss it.

Piper's response came slower this time.

I've got rehearsal this morning, but I
could get away for lunch. Is it okay if
my mom comes?

Sure. I'd love to meet her, too. Say
around noon?

Perfect. See you then!

"I could probably take my lunch early and join
you. If you don't want to go alone," Maggie offered.

"I appreciate that, but I think I should do this on
my own. Like you said, Ginny's is a very public place
and Ginny has my back."

At least I hope she did. My relationship with the
town's resident truth detector hadn't always been
good. My arrival had ruffled her feathers. At first, I
thought she didn't like me because I had magic. It
turned out she just wanted to be sure I didn't have ill
intentions towards the town. Over the last few
months, she'd warmed to me and I to her. Initially

I'd thought she was stuck up and snobby, but it was all a façade she played up.

"I should head back to the B&B and change," I said.

"I'd offer to make breakfast, but we both know it would pale in comparison to anything Tania's got on the stove."

Tania had been very into frittatas lately and the thought of them made my mouth water. I downed the rest of my coffee and rinsed the mug before giving Maggie a firm squeeze and kiss on the cheek.

"You're the best girlfriend I could have ever asked for," I told her.

"You're not half bad yourself," she teased. "Now go on, get out of here. You've got a very important date to keep."

Much to my relief, no one could see my borrowed attire as I made the short drive from Maggie's apartment to the B&B. In fact, much of the town appeared to be still asleep despite it being nearly nine o'clock on a Friday morning. Normally, I'd have been at work by now, but Sage was going out of town and had decided we all needed a paid three-day weekend.

So, I was left with three days off in a row.

I expected the driveway at the B&B to be filled

with cars. The way Sam had gone on about our next batch of guests, their arrival was imminent. Yet, I pulled into the usual spot the VW Bug occupied. I did notice depressions in the grass on either side of the drive, suggesting something had been parked there recently.

I headed inside to find Tania standing at the sink in the kitchen, washing dishes. She glanced my direction. "You stay at Maggie's last night?"

"Isn't it obvious?" Sam chirped from the other side of the room. "At least you had the decency to change clothes."

"Oh, quiet you," Tania chided.

Judging by the stack of plates she'd already washed, our additional guests had at least come through at some point. "Were you able to get everything you needed for the new guests?"

"I had to go to a market two towns over, but I think I got everything. I am happy for the business, but I have never dealt with someone having such particular tastes."

"Where are they?" I gestured to the empty space around us.

"They left for the day."

Sam gave a dramatic twirl and bow that put his torso through the kitchen table. "They're thespians."

Another coincidence?

"I can feel the mix of nerves and excitement coming off you in waves. What is going on?" Tania turned off the water, dried her hands on a dish rag, and turned to face me.

"I just found out I've got family here in the States. In New Hampshire actually. My Nan's sister moved here when she was young. Her daughter and granddaughter are still in the area."

"That's wonderful."

"I've made plans to meet up with Piper, that's Pauline's granddaughter, today at noon at Ginny's."

"How'd you convince her to come to you?" Sam interrupted.

"It turns out she's an actress and she's in some sort of troupe that's putting on a show here in town over the weekend."

"It sounds like she could be part of our group staying the weekend," Tania said.

Fear nagged at the back of my mind, that something was going to go wrong. It grew louder as I considered the possibility that we'd be sharing a living space while she was here in town.

"I didn't even know there was a show coming to town," I admitted as I rummaged in the cabinets for food.

Tania gestured for me to take a seat at the table, and she pulled a plate from the oven. She'd kept a plate of frittata for me. I mouthed a 'thank you' to her as I dug in.

"We sometimes have traveling shows come through town, but it usually isn't until summertime."

"They're a few months early," I pointed out. March had barely ended.

"For whatever reason they decided to come now, and I am not going to argue. But I will say it hasn't been as well publicized as some others."

I felt bad not having a real clue about what was happening in town. I had really started to think of myself as part of this community, but I still had some outsider habits to shake. I made a mental resolution to be better at keeping on top of the town's events from now on.

"Where do they do these productions?" I could see them being held down on the boardwalk in summer, but it was still too cold to hold them outdoors.

"We have a small theater off Pine Avenue," Tania explained.

Brookhaven was small enough to only have a handful of streets. They all appeared to branch off of Main Street. If memory served, Pine Avenue was in the opposite direction of High Time, and it snaked back behind the fire station and the school.

"I hope your first meeting goes well," Tania said as she patted my shoulder.

"Me, too."

"I hope she's not the whiny one who threw a fit all because the cheese wasn't the right type," Sam called as he flitted out of sight.

I wanted to say that couldn't have been Piper, but the truth was I had no idea what she might throw a fit over. A handful of messages over the internet weren't enough to know much of anything about her at all.

I resolved to get to Ginny's early. It would be better to be prepared for anything.

By a little before noon, I'd made myself presentable in a pair of jeans and a peasant top. I'd bound my hair into a knot at the nape of my neck. A few disagreeable curls fell to frame my face. I arrived at Ginny's just ahead of the lunch crowd and got a booth by the far wall with a clear view of the front door. I recognized a lot of the regulars' faces seated at the counter. The center stool was surprisingly empty. Ginny's absence made me uneasy.

"I told you we needed to be ready to move people through," Ginny's voice filtered from the back of the space.

I craned my neck to see the proprietor with her blonde hair in a high ponytail flung over her shoulder as she chastised one of the servers.

"But it's not even that busy," he argued.

"All of those theater people are going to eat somewhere," she replied. "So, tell Violet she's going to need to take her pie to go today. And Gerry can't have his booth all afternoon."

I caught the server mutter, "Why can't you tell them ...?" But Ginny had already walked away and made her way to the table where I sat.

"We're going to need this booth soon," she said matter-of-factly.

"I'm actually waiting for a few people to join me," I answered. All of a sudden, I wasn't sure why, but felt compelled to explain further. "It's some relatives I just discovered." Maybe it was Ginny's ability to pull the truth from people at work.

Without invitation, Ginny dropped into the seat across from me. "I don't want to interrupt a family reunion." Her perky expression faltered. "It's no secret I'm not exactly the world's biggest fan of people coming through my town."

"Look at it this way, they're going to be bringing in more business for the whole town. That can't be a bad thing."

"Strangers in town always means there's a chance something is going to go wrong."

She'd spent her whole life in town, so she clearly had more experience with this sort of event. "Maybe it won't be so bad this time around."

"Cling to that optimism, Darcy," she said as she patted my hand before standing and moving to shoo Gerry from his booth.

I glanced across the café to watch him fold up his newspaper and head out. He caught me watching and gave me a polite head nod. It had been nearly five months since Gerry's only son had been murdered by his own daughter for the abuse he'd inflicted on her mother and his string of other ex-wives. I'd been impressed with how quickly the town moved on from such a scandal, especially as there wasn't much else newsworthy happening in the small town.

As the regulars filtered out to make way for the theater crowd, I turned my attention to the front door. I'd only skimmed a few of Piper's photos on

Facebook, but I'd been seeking ones that showed her mother as well. Hopefully, it meant I had a better chance of recognizing them when they arrived.

A few minutes later the door swung open, and two women walked in. As I looked at them, they had that vague familiarity of having seen photos of them before. The younger one pulled out a phone, studied the screen, and looked around. Her gaze landed on me, and I was halfway out of my seat by the time they had reached the table.

"Darcy?" Her voice came out with an excited squeak.

"Piper?" I answered and she threw her arms around me.

"It's so good to meet you," she said and gave me a bear hug. When she finally relinquished her grip, she pointed to the older woman standing off to the side. "This is my mom."

"Audrey, right?" I said, holding out a hand.

"Someone's done her research," Audrey said, giving my hand a light shake.

"Mom, stop," Piper chided as she slid into the other side of the booth.

"I don't blame you for being tentative. I was a bit nervous this morning myself," I said. I pulled up the information from Nan on my phone and showed it to her. "My Nan, Pauline's sister, sent this to me yesterday. It's what led me to tracking you both down online."

She studied it and the tension eased in her neck muscles. She sat down. "You must have questions."

"I do. But I have to know, did your side of the family inherit Pauline's magic?"

4

———

*A*udrey's cheeks paled and she looked around the café, as if she feared we would be overheard. That suggested the answer to my question was yes.

"This town's pretty open about the existence of magic," I said, hoping to put her mind at ease. "No one's going to look at us funny for bandying the word about."

"I told you this place was cool with it," Piper declared, giving her mother a look that said, 'stop being paranoid.'

"It just isn't something we talk about in public," Audrey said.

"Yes, we've got magic. Grammy says its heredi- tary," Piper explained, leaning with her elbows on the table. "But I guess you probably knew that already."

"To be honest, until a few months ago, I didn't even know it was a possibility. I came into my powers and my parents weren't exactly supportive. It's partly why I ended up here in the States."

"What can you do?" Piper's eyes were wide in anticipation.

"I can sort of talk to plants. It's hard to explain, but it's like they've got a voice only I can hear. I can see and feel their potential. Oh, and I can help them grow." They both gaped at me. "Okay, I realize that does sound a bit mental."

"Have you always been drawn to plants?" Audrey's question came with a pensive expression.

"Not that I can recall. I mean, it wasn't like I had a black thumb or anything, but it wasn't like I purposely surrounded myself with plants. Why, is that how it manifested for you?"

"I was always into candles as a kid. Even when I shouldn't have been. Mom got worried I was going to turn into a pyro," Piper said with a small laugh. "Guess in a way, she was right."

"What about your uncles? Do you know what sort of magic they had?"

"We didn't really talk about it much as children,

but I think they were both more linked to emotions," Audrey answered quiet."

"Grandma said it was the same for her when she was growing up. She was always drawn to the earth. Maybe that's where your magic comes from," Piper explained.

"I'm sorry, this is making me feel a bit uncomfortable," Audrey interrupted her daughter. "Why don't you tell us what you do for a living, Darcy?"

"Uh, well, I work at the town's marijuana dispensary, tending the plants. It's really the perfect job for me, given my ... abilities." The server Ginny had been chastising earlier came by the table. We ordered food and coffee.

"What about you? You said you were traveling with a troupe? I know we've got a play in town for the weekend."

"That's us," Piper answered, some of the vigor fading from her tone. "It's a semi-professional Shakespeare company. You've probably seen the posters around town. We're doing Romeo and Juliet."

"It's going to sound awful, but I was never a big Shakespeare fan. Bloke took too many words to say things," I said.

"He's an acquired taste for sure," Piper replied.

"Piper has a very important role," Audrey insisted.

"Actually, I'm just one of the lighting technicians," she answered. "I mean, one day I'll be on stage, but I doubt it will be this one."

"Well, you aren't going to get there with that attitude," Audrey chided. "She's being modest. Her part is really important, she's the female lead's understudy."

"You've got to be really good to get that," I said, hoping I hadn't just insulted her.

"It means I'm not quite good enough," Piper said, sinking back against the booth as the server brought her coffee. She wrapped her hands around the over-sized mug—like the one Ginny usually sported— and turned her attention to the contents within.

"She just needs to work on her confidence," Audrey said, eyeing her daughter.

"Are you only staying in town for the duration of the play?" I broached, trying to change the subject.

"We've got shows in Maine after this. Then back over to New Hampshire to wrap up the tour," Piper replied. "Not a lot of time for sight-seeing or just hanging out."

"Well, we'll have to keep in touch. Now that we're connected online, that should be easy." I took a bite of my sandwich. "You know, we'll probably see each other after the shows anyway. You're all staying at Tia Tania's B&B, right?"

"How'd you know?" Piper asked.

"She's technically my landlady. I came here on a holiday about a year ago and stayed there. When I moved here for good, she offered me a permanent room."

"She's very accommodating," Audrey said.

The look Piper gave her mother suggested there was more to the story. When Piper realized I'd noticed, she said, "The lead in the play, Janice Farley, is kind of extra. She freaks out over everything."

"Oh, that explains the specialty food Tania picked up."

"I'm glad we'll get to hang out around the shows," Piper said.

"You know, the troupe gives Piper a couple of free tickets to the show whenever they land in a venue. Even if Shakespeare's not your usual thing, why not come see the show?" Audrey's eyes sparkled as she spoke. Like she hoped her enthusiasm would rub off on me.

Is that her power?

"I'd love to." The words tumbled from my lips

before I could think through the response. "Is it okay if I bring a date?"

That perked Piper up. "Of course."

"Grand. I'll have to make sure she's free tonight."

Piper's phone beeped at her, cutting the interaction short. "I've got to get back. There's something wrong with the equipment."

"What time's the show tonight?" I asked, as she scooted past her mother.

"Curtain is at seven o'clock."

"We'll be there," I said.

Audrey stood to let Piper exit and gave her daughter a quick hug before sitting back down in the booth. As Piper rushed out of the café, I noticed a few unfamiliar faces tracking her movements. Yet, none of them went after her.

"So, are the tickets something I need to go to the theater to pick up?" I prompted.

"What? Oh, no they're digital. I can email them to you."

I gave her my email and we sat finishing our meals. "I'm sorry if I made things weird earlier. I didn't mean to upset you."

"Oh, you didn't. I am the one who should be apologizing. It's just not something we talk about in public." She gestured to the surrounding area.

"We don't come from a community as open as this."

"I'd love to talk to you more about it, maybe after the show or sometime while you're staying at the B&B?"

"Sure." She set her knife and fork down, pushing the remnants of her salad aside. "This was all very sudden ... family showing up out of the blue is a bit of a touchy subject for me personally."

"Can I ask why?"

"I don't know if you're aware, but I had two older brothers."

"I saw their names on the family tree my Nan sent. It showed they both died during military deployments. My condolences."

"Well, there was a scam a few years ago. It involved a woman claiming she was Patrick's child by a woman he'd met overseas. It ended badly."

"Oh ... So, when I showed up out of nowhere, it set your defenses off."

"Yes."

"I understand. If you want to do a DNA test or whatever, I'd be up for it. I want this to be a relationship I can nurture, but that needs to go both ways. We both need to be comfortable."

"How about for now, we just enjoy the play?"

"I think I can manage that."

Now I just had to convince Maggie to join me.

I DIDN'T HAVE to try very hard to convince Maggie to be my plus one. Apparently, she was a closet Shakespeare lover. I'd prefaced the invitation with the declaration that I knew very little about the bard or most of his plays. Luckily, I'd been forced to read Romeo and Juliet in a literature class at university.

"I promise I won't be that obnoxious person who gets up in arms when they take liberties with the dialogue," Maggie promised as we strolled arm in arm down Pine Avenue toward the theater.

"Good," I teased.

The theater was one of the taller buildings in town. It was a two-story structure with a pale pink brick façade with white trimmed windows and a dark roof. There was a stylized poster showcasing Romeo and Juliet secured inside the front window. It promised a Friday evening performance along with two shows each on Saturday and Sunday. Given that I hadn't heard many people talking about it, I questioned whether having so many shows was a wise financial decision.

The single-story fire station sat across the road. I'd seen a few of the fire fighters come through Ginny's when I was there and even caught a couple making purchases at High Time. Beyond that though, I hadn't had an occasion to interact with the fire department. Even when I'd found myself entangled with dead bodies, it was always Chief Hayes or Vinnie who came to the scene.

To my surprise there was a line to get into the theater when we arrived. We wound our way to the back of the cue. As we inched forward, I started to get a glimpse of the interior.

"I wouldn't have thought this would be so popular," I told Maggie as we stepped up to the front entrance.

"Darcy, you've lived here long enough now to know we don't have that much entertainment in the winter months. We take our thrills where we can get them," she said with a smirk.

I showed the ticket taker the confirmation on my phone, and he waved us inside. The lobby was covered in thick burgundy carpeting. Faux support columns flanked the doors to the theater. I spotted staircases in the same burgundy material winding up to a second level of seating. I led the way to the main floor. The seats we'd been assigned were in the middle of the center section. It was actually a decent seating reservation. It afforded us a clear view of the entire stage and I could even look up into the balcony level. I turned toward the back and spotted Piper in the lighting booth with a headset on. She sat next to a man in glasses who looked deep in conversation with her. In short order the theater had filled to capacity, and I settled against the deep blue cushion. The curtains opened on the stage and the play began.

By the time intermission hit, I recalled why I wasn't a fan of this particular play. The bloody dialogue was just so confusing. At least Maggie appeared to be enjoying herself. We stepped out into the lobby to stretch our legs and I heard footsteps thundering down the stairs to my right. Piper appeared with her headset slung around her neck.

"You made it!"

"I said I would be happy to come," I said. "The lighting looks really good."

"Thanks." She gestured to Maggie. "Want to introduce me to your date?"

Maggie slid her hand into mine. "I'm Maggie, Darcy's girlfriend."

"Piper, her cousin like twice removed or something?"

"Cousin works," I said. There wasn't a need to overcomplicate it.

"I've really enjoyed the cast so far," Maggie said.

Heat flushed my whole body. I'd forgotten to tell Maggie about Piper's understudy status. "Piper is actually the understudy for Juliet."

Just then, a voice crackled over the radio on her hip. "Piper, we're missing props for the next scene."

Piper let out an irritated huff. "You'd think we didn't have a prop department." She plucked the radio from her belt. "I'll be right there."

"You better go save the day, cousin," I said.

My words brought a smile to her lips as she darted out of view. Maggie and I strolled the short length of the lobby. "She seemed nice," Maggie offered.

"Yeah. Her mum's a bit skittish with talking about magic. But they're staying at the B&B, so I'm hopeful we'll get to talk more about it before they head out of town."

"Good. I'm glad you're getting to connect with a piece of your heritage."

The lights around us dimmed twice, signaling that intermission was over. We retreated to the theater and reclaimed our seats. As the curtain pulled back again to reveal the actors with a new scenic backdrop, I wondered what prop emergency had pulled Piper away.

I tried to lose myself in the story, but it was hard to get invested when I knew the tragedy about to befall the characters. I couldn't imagine being willing to take my own life in the name of love. The actor playing Romeo had already pretended to drink the poison and lay motionless on the stage.

The theater fell quiet as Janice sat up from where she'd lain, pretending to be dead. I didn't pay attention to the words she spoke as she moved, throwing herself around the stage in overacted grief. She pulled the sword from Romeo's belt and moved to plunge it into her heart. I sat up as I was keen to see if she did the old theater trick of shoving it under her arm or if they used a retractable blade for the stunt.

Almost immediately something felt off. Janice's eyes went wide, and she dropped the sword without making any move to stab herself. She raised her hands to her face and her eyes went wide. The sword clattered to the wooden stage with a deafening clank as she staggered backwards. Her face grew red and blotchy, and I could see her fingers swelling along with her cheeks.

"She's milking it a bit, isn't she? I thought she was

supposed to stab herself." a woman in the row behind me said louder than necessary.

I turned to Maggie. "Something's wrong," I said in a strained tone.

Onstage, Janice let out a gargle that was picked up by the microphone as she slumped over. Maggie didn't need to be told twice. She was out of her seat and racing toward the front of the theater before the other actors even had time to make their entrance for the next scene.

"What are you doing?" Someone in the front shouted.

"Get off the stage," someone else called.

Maggie ignored them both. She climbed onto the edge of the stage and moved to Janice's side, probing her throat, and turning her face toward the ceiling. "We need paramedics. She's not breathing!" Maggie's voice rang out clear through the space.

Panic erupted in the theater as cast members flocked to the stage. I'd moved out of my seat and into the aisle. I caught sight of Ginny a few rows back, phone pressed to ear. I had no doubt she was phoning the Chief of Police. I just hoped he would bring an ambulance with him.

I turned my attention back to the stage as Maggie began chest compressions, trying to get Janice breathing again. By the painful expression on her face, I had a sinking feeling that the ambulance wouldn't be needed after all.

Commotion from behind me pulled my gaze from Maggie to reveal Chief Hayes barreling down the aisle, two paramedics in tow. They rushed to the stage and ushered Maggie out of the way. She scooted off the stage, but stayed near the front of the space to share whatever insights she had into Janice's condition.

Maggie was a healer by profession and by magical skill, but even she couldn't revive the dead. I swallowed the lump in my throat as I looked up at the booth where Piper sat. I could just make out the look of horror on her face as the realization settled over the crowd, that yet another person had died here in Brookhaven. And that meant another investigation. Maybe I'd get lucky and stay out of it this time. Yeah, I wouldn't have that sort of luck.

5

An uneasy silence settled over the theater as the medics moved Janice onto a gurney, one straddling her torso to continue chest compressions while the other maneuvered them up the aisle. I took several deep breaths to keep myself from sprinting past them to Maggie's side. Up on the stage, Chief Hayes spoke with a black-clad person, a stagehand who handed him a microphone.

"Ladies and gentlemen, I am sorry to have to cut the evening short, but the rest of tonight's entertainment is cancelled." His voice boomed in the confined space and the speakers squealed with feedback.

"Is she going to be okay?" a woman a few rows in front of me called out.

"I'm afraid I can't answer that. But I am going to need everyone to stay in their seats until either myself or my deputy has had a chance to take your statement."

A collective groan went up from the crowd at his words. It made sense though. Janice had collapsed under unusual circumstances. And it was possible any one of us could have seen something that could provide clarity about what had happened. Chief Hayes returned the microphone and leapt off the stage, phone already pressed to his ear. He hurried up the aisle past me. He slowed just enough for me to hear him on the phone with Vinnie, his deputy.

"I know it's your night off, but I need you at the theater. There's been an incident."

He exited the theater into the lobby, probably to wait for Vinnie's arrival. I'd turned my phone to silent for the show, but saw now I had a missed message from Tania only a few minutes ago. I didn't bother listening to it. Instead, I redialed her number and did my best not to draw attention to myself.

"Darcy, what is going on?" Tania's voice came over the line after the first ring.

"There's been an accident at the theater. The lead actress, Janice, collapsed on stage," I relayed as quietly as possible.

"*Dios mio*," she murmured. "That explains the ambulance I saw."

"Chief Hayes is going to interview everyone. I have a bad feeling about this."

"I am the one who usually gets those," she said in a half-hearted joking tone.

"I'll keep you updated if I hear anything. But I don't imagine the cast and crew will be back to the B&B until late."

"I appreciate you letting me know."

I ended the call and glanced back toward the lobby where Chief Hayes stood talking to one of the ushers. Vinnie had yet to make an appearance. I didn't plan to leave the theater and I highly doubted Chief Hayes would make me his next interview. So, I climbed past the older gentleman seated at the end of the row and moved down the aisle toward the stage as unobtrusively as possible.

Maggie sat in one of the empty front row seats, staring at her hands. I slid into the vacant seat beside her and tried to take her hands in mine. She pulled away, looking up at me with a frightened expression.

"You did what you could," I told her.

"It was so strange," Maggie whispered before looking down at her hands again. "It looked like she was having a reaction to something, but there was nothing there."

"I'm sure Chief Hayes will get it sorted." I was more worried about her demeanor. I'd never seen her look this spooked, not even when she'd been accused of murder and hauled away in handcuffs six months ago. "Maggie, look at me. You did everything you could. You know that, right?"

Slowly, she nodded, tightening her hands into fists. "Sorry, just not feeling particularly confident in my healing abilities at the moment."

"All of our magic has limits."

"I know you're trying to cheer me up," she said.

"Is it working?"

"Weirdly, kind of."

We shared a small laugh just as the doors at the back of the theater opened and Chief Hayes returned with Vinnie. I watched as the chief directed Vinnie in our direction. Maybe if we could get our statements out of the way, we would be permitted to leave. After all, I had a feeling Tania was going to need help corralling the actors and crew, especially knowing one of their own was in dire straits.

Vinnie reached the stage and gestured to the stagehand to give him microphone the chief had used earlier. "Ladies and gentlemen, we will be working our way to the middle so please be patient. Once we've taken your statement, you are free to go," he explained.

He passed the mic back to the stagehand before he approached Maggie and I. "Rick said you were with the victim when he arrived?"

Maggie cleared her throat and rose to her feet. "Yes."

"Why don't you tell me what happened?" He made eye contact with me and offered a small head nod to signal he acknowledged my presence.

I stood and moved away to give them some privacy, although I was still close enough to catch much of the conversation.

"It was almost the end of the play. Romeo had committed suicide and Juliet was about to do the same," Maggie explained. "But when the actress playing Juliet picked up the sword, it was like she had some sort of reaction, an allergy."

"And you could see this? Where were you sitting?"

"Middle of the center section. And yes, it was pretty obvious."

"And given your medical background, you tried to help her."

"I tried."

"Thanks." Vinnie pivoted to look at me. "Darcy, I can take your statement now, too."

I stepped up. "I'm not sure what else I can offer that Maggie couldn't tell you. We were sitting next to each other."

"Oh, so you were here together?"

"Yeah. It was a date." The ease with which the last word left my mouth made me momentarily giddy. "It was sort of last minute. I got the tickets earlier today."

"You did? I heard they were sold out."

"I guess the cast and crew gets a few free tickets to hand out and we got them that way."

"This is a traveling show. Do you know someone in the cast?"

"Funny story, it turns out I've got a cousin who lives in New Hampshire and is in the crew. Piper Hennessey." I gestured toward the lighting booth. "She's handling the lights."

"And you didn't notice anything unusual before the incident?"

"No. We talked to Piper for a couple of minutes during intermission, but she got called away."

"Do you remember what for?"

"Something about a prop. I'm not sure exactly, if I'm honest."

"Thanks." He gestured between Maggie and me. "You two are free to head out."

"Thanks, Vinnie," Maggie said.

He moved off to speak with some of the other audience members in the front of the theater. I watched Chief Hayes at the back, speaking with some of the patrons who'd been seated behind us.

"Do you have any idea what could have caused her to have that kind of reaction?" I asked as we made our way along the far wall and out to the lobby.

"It looked almost like some sort of allergic reaction. But from what, I couldn't tell."

As we made our way to the lobby, I could hear voices arguing from the staircase to our left. It sounded like Piper and another female voice. I held out a hand to stop Maggie from leaving.

"... what happened?" the first voice said.

"I don't know. But I know how it's going to look," Piper answered, her voice getting louder as they descended the stairs. "They were having trouble with the sword during intermission."

Well, that answered one question I'd been contemplating. So, Piper had gone to fiddle with the sword after talking to us. I could also see how that would make her look bad, especially if something with the sword had led to Janice's condition.

"No one would think anything bad about you," the other voice, who I now recognized as Audrey, insisted.

They came into view and stopped talking as soon as they spotted Maggie and I standing there. It took both women a moment to recognize that we weren't law enforcement. Piper opened her mouth to say something, but a firm arm squeeze from Audrey kept her quiet.

"Sorry, everything went so wrong tonight. I'd really hoped our first meeting would have been less … dramatic," Piper finally offered just as Chief Hayes appeared, gesturing for the pair of them to step into the theater to give their statements.

Maggie led the way out of the theater and into the evening air. It was brisk now that the sun had set. She looked more with it and was aware of her surroundings. Or maybe the shock of Janice's collapse was starting to lessen. I looped my arm through hers as we made our way slowly back toward the B&B.

"Did you hear what Piper said to her mum while they were coming down the stairs?" I broached.

"No. I wasn't really paying attention," she admitted.

"She said it could look bad since they'd called her back to fix the sword before the play resumed. That's not a detail the police are likely to miss."

"Well, she'll have to explain whatever she was doing with it," Maggie said.

"She was Janice's understudy, too."

"Darcy, I can tell you've got a theory brewing, so just tell me what you're thinking."

I'd gotten myself in trouble in the past by assuming the worst of people. But, if even Piper was pointing out things that made her look questionable, I couldn't simply ignore it. "She was Janice's understudy. And I got the sense from talking to her and Audrey that Audrey wasn't pleased by that. She didn't want Piper stuck doing the lighting."

"Do you think she did something to the sword to get Janice out of the way, so she could have her moment in the spotlight?"

"I don't know. Maybe. I don't know her well enough to say one way or the other. But she's not wrong that it makes her look like someone Chief Hayes ought to be focusing on."

"She might be family, Darcy, but that doesn't mean you've to get involved," Maggie reminded me.

I could picture Nan's face racked with disappointment if she found out I'd just left Piper hanging. We might not know each other well, but I'd been the one to reach out to her. I'd initiated contact and couldn't shake the feeling that I owed it to Nan to keep an eye out for my cousin, even if that meant digging around the investigation and putting myself in Chief Hayes' crosshairs.

"I know I don't have to," I mumbled.

"But you're going to," she confirmed.

"You said it yourself, something seemed off about what happened to Janice. And you looked really out of it afterward."

"I felt sort of out of it. It was like for a couple of minutes, all I could think about was the fact I'd failed. That I wasn't worthy of being called a healer."

"I know I'm your girlfriend and duty bound to remind you that you are a bloody good healer, but it's the truth, Maggie. You are brilliant at what you do. Don't ever think you're a failure."

"Thanks for that." We continued on for a few paces, the sign for High Time coming into view to our left. "The thing is ... I don't think I've ever really told anyone this before ... but being a failure at the one thing I was literally gifted to do has always been my greatest fear. And after I'd stopped working on

Janice and the paramedics took over, it was as if that fear hit me tenfold."

"But you're okay now?" I prompted.

"Yeah. A little shaken, but it's mostly subsided."

"Good. I'm sure Tania will insist you come in for some tea. I suspect she's feeling quite a lot of intense emotions right now."

"I'm not sure she needs my insecurity," she said.

We reached the front door of the B&B and on cue, Tania opened the door. The worry lines around her mouth and eyes were deep. "I could sense the two of you walking up the street. This isn't just an accident, is it?"

"We don't know anything more than what I told you before. The female lead collapsed on stage. The paramedics took her out on a gurney. Vinnie took our statements, and we were able to leave," I explained in one long breath.

"I've already got some of Maggie's special chamomile tea steeping," she said.

"While that sounds really nice, I think I'm just going to head home," Maggie insisted. "You're going to have a lot of really stressed out actors and crewmembers soon enough. You don't need me hanging around right now."

Tania offered a sympathetic nod and returned

inside. I pulled Maggie into a tight embrace. "Call me if you need anything."

"I will. I promise." She sealed it with a brief kiss before she pulled away and headed down the front steps.

I moved into the front hall and eased the door shut behind me. I followed the soothing scent of the tea into the kitchen to find Tania had already prepared a tray of sandwiches in anticipation of the cast's return.

"You still have that bad feeling," Tania stated matter-of-factly.

"The way Piper was talking, she knew the police were going to look at her as a person of interest. And I have to admit it feels like she could have a motive."

"But you don't know her well enough to make that judgment call."

One brief coffee together was certainly not enough to claim I knew her. "It just feels like more than a coincidence that this is all happening here in Brookhaven. It's almost like the universe put us in each other's orbits for a reason.

Tania poured some tea into two mugs and handed me one. "Who are we to argue with the universe? But I can tell you right now, Rick isn't going to like you looking into this."

"Believe me, I know. Things have been going so well the last few months. I don't want to ruin it. I'm going to do my best to stay out of his way."

Besides, he couldn't stop me from talking to people here at the B&B. I took a fortifying sip of tea and readied myself for the theater troupe's inevitable arrival.

6

It was well after midnight by the time the troupe began staggering through the door. I'd only managed to stay up thanks to some extra strong coffee, but even that was wearing off now. My plans to see what I could glean from the cast and crew would have to wait until a more respectable hour.

I crawled beneath the sheets and fell into a fitful sleep. Janice's strange reaction played out in a loop in my dreams. Sometimes the sword turned out to be real and she ended up accidentally impaling herself. And perhaps even more horrifying, sometimes when Maggie went to render aid, she too wound up lying stabbed on the stage. By the time my phone alarm went off at seven o'clock, a thin layer of cold sweat coated me from head to toe. Shivering, I grabbed clean clothes and darted for the bathroom, shower caddy slung over my shoulder.

I stayed sequestered in the shower far longer than usual. I let the warmth soak into my skin and wash away the stress of the night before. I stood wrapped in a towel as the time ticked past seven thirty, and began to formulate a plan. My first order of business was checking in on Maggie. I wasn't one for prophetic dreams, but I still couldn't dismiss the dread that had woken me this morning. I needed to know she was okay. Once I'd ensured my girlfriend's well-being, I would pay Piper a visit. I needed to know why she thought she might be a suspect. And then, with any luck the police would have information that would explain the whole strange affair.

The rest of the B&B was quiet as I padded downstairs to the kitchen. Not even Tania was up and about, which set my nerves on edge. She was always an early riser, especially when we had guests. I started the coffee pot and dialed Maggie's number, pressing the phone to my ear.

The line rang three times before Maggie answered with a sleepy, "He-Hello?"

"Oh, bugger, I'm an idiot. Of course, you're still sleeping," I rambled.

"Darcy, what's going on?" The sleep faded from Maggie's tone.

"I just wanted to check on you after last night. You had me worried." I didn't want to burden her with my nightmares.

"I had some herbal tea and it helped calm things. I think I'm still a little shaken, but mostly better. How's everyone at the B&B?"

"Sleeping still. Most didn't start getting back until after midnight."

"I'm sure Rick and Vinnie are exhausted."

"What do you think happened on stage last night?"

"I really can't say. But I know it felt like ..." she trailed off.

"Felt like what?"

"It's going to sound ridiculous, but it felt like there was magic in the air."

"We live in a supernatural town and we're witches. That's not ridiculous at all."

"Good point." After a moment she added, "It just felt like something was there and it wasn't supposed to be there."

"Well, hopefully Chief Hayes found out what happened, and we won't have to worry about it," I offered as much to assuage her concerns as my own.

"Just promise me you won't get mixed up in things, Darcy."

"I'm trying not to. I swear," I replied just as I heard footsteps in the hall just beyond the kitchen. "I'll stop by in a bit."

"You're sweet."

The words 'I love you' caught on the tip of my tongue, but I held them back. We'd only been dating a few months. We were decidedly not at the 'l' word yet. "Go back to bed," I said instead and ended the call.

The coffee pot began to percolate, rumbling just as the footsteps moved from the front hall into the kitchen. Piper looked like she hadn't slept much. She looked surprised to see me standing there.

"You must have had an absolutely horrible night," I said and crossed the space to pull down two coffee mugs from the cabinet beside the oven.

"I still can't believe Janice is in the hospital," she replied, accepting the cup once I'd poured the steaming liquid into the mug for her. She didn't give me a chance to offer milk or sweetener before she took a long pull from it.

That suggested the answer to one of my questions. "The police took my statement pretty early on and I left. Do you have any idea what might have happened?"

Piper studied the contents of her cup in silence for a long while. "I didn't see much from up in the lighting booth."

"And nothing like this has happened on the tour before?" I probed as gently as possible. I could feel myself being pulled into the weeds of Janice's malady.

"No." she began pacing the length of the kitchen, mug still clutched firmly between her hands. "The scene has played out exactly like it's supposed to. She pretends to stab herself with the sword, she falls to the ground and then Romeo wakes up and drinks the poison."

I could feel her holding back information and part of me couldn't blame her. Even though we're cousins, I was still very much a stranger to her and her to me. "I didn't get a good look when I was near the stage, but is the sword supposed to be retractable?"

"Yeah. Except someone had been fiddling with it. Our prop guys aren't what you would call gentle on the weaponry, and they'd managed to jam it into the extended position."

"Is that why you were called back right before the intermission ended?"

She nodded and waggled the fingers of her right hand at me. "They claim I've got more nimble fingers. Honestly, I think they're just lazy."

"And you didn't notice anything off about it when you went to fix it?"

Her gaze narrowed as suspicion sharpened the angles of her nose and cheekbones. "Why so many questions?"

"Just trying to piece together what could have happened to occupy my mind. Seeing someone collapse like that is pretty frightening."

The tension eased from her expression. "I guess that's a natural thing to do."

"I didn't mean anything by it, really. When strange things happen, I kind of can't help but try to sort out the how."

"See a lot of strange things around here?"

"More than you'd expect," I admitted.

Piper set her now empty mug on the counter and glanced around the kitchen. "I don't want to be that guest, but I kind of thought meals were included."

"I think Tania's having a lie in today. Everyone's pretty shaken by what happened at the show. But I know that Ginny's does a mean breakfast. Come on, my treat."

"Lead the way."

Secretly, I hoped Ginny would be holding court in her usual spot. Maybe just being in the woman's proximity would encourage Piper to open up.

THE CAFÉ WAS MOSTLY empty when we arrived. Sunday mornings were typically booming with business and regulars. My stomach dropped when I saw Ginny's seat at the center of the counter vacant. The worry faded as the door between the restaurant and the kitchen swung open. The eponymous owner appeared; her blonde hair slicked back in a tight bun.

"You can sit anywhere," she said.

I picked a spot toward the end of the counter and Piper took up residence to my right. Ginny rounded the space and set down menus in front of us.

"I thought she owned this place," Piper noted in a hushed tone.

"And that means I can't take orders?" Ginny quipped, clearly hearing her words.

"Of course not. I just ... I'm surprised that's all."

"Hard work is what keeps this town running," Ginny continued. "I know it may look like I sit on my butt all day and gossip, but I take care of the people in this town."

I gave her no argument. With no one to challenge her statements, the bluster faded, and she disappeared back into the kitchen. We browsed the menus in silence for a while.

"Can I ask you something else?" I finally broached.

Piper set down her menu and swiveled on the stool to face me. "Sure."

"You and your mum were pretty surprised that magic is so openly practiced here. Were you the only person with magic in the cast and crew?"

"As far as I know. Why?"

I shook my head. "It could be nothing. It's just, Maggie said she felt magic in the theater. Well actually on the stage, when Janice went down."

"You think whatever happened was caused by magic?"

"Like I said, I've seen some pretty strange things since moving to this town and a lot of it was magic based."

Piper rubbed at her temple deep in thought as Ginny reappeared carrying a coffee pot and three oversized mugs stacked one on top of the other. Artfully, she set them down on the counter, filling each one of them to the brim.

"I have a feeling you're going to need this," she said, pushing one toward Piper.

"Thanks." She took a sip and turned back to me. "I really don't think I noticed anything unusual before everything happened."

"I heard one of the paramedics talk about getting an EpiPen," Ginny offered unsolicited.

"An allergic reaction?" Under normal circumstances I would have said that seemed far-fetched. But Janice had some sort of food allergy. At least that much I already knew.

"I mean, she's deathly allergic to peanuts," Piper said. "But everyone in the troupe knew that and all of us were really careful not to even look at them."

"And you're sure you didn't notice anything off about the prop sword when you were fixing it?"

"Like I said before, one of the prop guys got the sword stuck in the extended position. I got it retracted properly, but I didn't notice anything off about it."

"Having something be such a well-known weakness seems like a pretty easy means to take her out of the picture," Ginny said, eyeing me.

"I know Tania was taking precautions at the B&B to avoid any possible cross-contamination."

"And aside from that little break where my mom and I came to have coffee with you, we were in rehearsal all day. We didn't even have time for real food."

"Did anyone leave, even for just a few minutes? They could have picked up something from one of the shops on Main Street," I suggested.

"Not that I saw. But I was busy with Benji, making sure everything was set for the lighting. I guess some of the make-up department could have gone out, but I'm telling you Janice was paranoid about what she ate. And she wasn't ever quiet when she thought people were putting her at risk."

"Not that I want to rush paying customers, but you should really eat something." Ginny directed her comment at Piper.

What does she know?

"Oh, uh, I guess I'll take the French toast plate. No powdered sugar."

"I'll just take some fried eggs and a side of toast and jam," I added.

Ginny snapped up the menus and disappeared into the kitchen again, leaving Piper and I to sit in awkward silence.

"So, what exactly can you do with your magic?" Piper redirected the conversation.

"Oh, well, I sort of hear plants. It's not words really. Not like how you'd normally think of communicating. But I can hear the promise of what they will become. I can influence their growth. Oh, and I can even use it defensively." Images of conjuring latticework barriers from the grass in the yard at Tania's came to mind. "But I'm still so new at it I'm sure there's loads I haven't figured out yet."

"Must have been scary to realize there was something different about you."

"Terrifying actually. Your mum said you exhibited your powers young?"

"Not exactly. I was always interested in candles, fireworks, anything with fire really. My mom thought it was just a weird obsession. She even worried I might turn out to be some kind of crazy pyro kid. But it was just my magic trying to exert itself."

"So, you can do things with fire. I met a witch who can harness water so that makes sense."

"I'll be honest, it freaked my mom out the first time I accidentally stuck my hand in a flame and didn't get burned. She took me to the doctor, because she thought maybe I was a hemophiliac or something. But there was nothing wrong with me."

"It's pretty remarkable isn't it, how magic can manifest in such different ways in one family. My Nan can sort of see the future. Not at all like what we can do."

"I guess it must follow some sort of law of nature. Why not the general rules of genetics ... that different combinations of DNA result in all the many ways magic shows up?" Piper said.

The door of the kitchen swung open again and Ginny returned to set our plates on the counter in front of us. She slid a receipt under my plate. I passed over a couple of twenty dollar bills to cover the cost including tip and tucked into my meal.

I'd just set down my fork and knife when the bell above the front door behind us rang, announcing a new patron. The fact that Ginny didn't move to greet them or direct them to a table set my nerves on edge. Piper appeared oblivious to her surroundings as she took her last bite of breakfast. I did a quarter turn on my stool and my stomach dropped, threatening the food I'd just eaten to make a reappearance. Chief Hayes stood there staring intently at Piper. I could see the dark circles under his eyes. He was a man who had not slept at all. And the way he toyed with the clip securing the handcuffs on his belt suggested he'd come here for a reason.

"Piper Hennessey?" His voice betrayed the exhaustion he clearly felt.

Piper turned and nearly fell off the stool at the sight of the police chief standing there before her. "Yes?" It came out as a squeak.

"I'm going to need you to come down to the station to answer some more questions."

"But I gave you my statement last night," she protested.

He glanced at me, but I stayed still and silent like a statue. He took a step closer, dropping his hands to his sides. "Circumstances have changed, and you need to come answer further questions. I'd prefer if you came along voluntarily."

Piper turned to me, her face stricken with fear. On instinct, I reached out a hand and gave hers a firm squeeze. "It's just some questions. It would be best if you cooperate and go answer them."

I knew better than to ask to escort her to the station. It would be met with downright refusal. However, that didn't mean I had no way of spying on their conversation. Piper's fingers trembled beneath my own as she pulled them free. I could see the true fear in her eyes as she tried to straighten up and face the situation head on. Being called down to the station for more questions spooked her.

"Okay. I'll come with you."

"Don't worry, I'll let your mum know you'll be back soon," I called to her as Chief Hayes led my cousin away from the café and out of sight.

Now I just had to make it back to the B&B, convince my favorite chameleon to lend a hand, and get to the station before they started questioning Piper.

So much for staying out of this mess.

7

’d never run so fast in my life. I made it back to the front steps of the B&B in under two minutes. Not bothering to stop to catch my breath, I barreled up the stairs to my bedroom. Beau had been keeping to himself since the troupe had arrived. Like Sam, he tended to stay out of sight when there were mundane guests in the house. But he’d been snoozing on my pillow when I’d gotten up this morning.

I ran a hand across what should have been the soft surface of the pillowcase, only to find it covered with the leathery bumps and ridges of reptilian scales. “Sorry to wake you, mate, but I need your help,” I said gasping.

A ripple in the air revealed Beau. He cracked one

eye open to stare at me. He then opened his other eye and uncurled himself, arching into a small stretch that looked more like it belonged to a feline rather than a reptile and crawled up my arm.

"Piper's in trouble and I need to see what the police have on her. So, I'm going to need you to hide me."

'Dangerous risk for strangers.'

I heard his voice echo in my head.

"I know, but she's family and I'm not going to lose this one, too. So please, help me out?"

'Help family.'

"Thank you," I whispered, before darting back down the stairs.

"Darcy, is that you?" Tania's voice called from the kitchen.

"Sorry, can't talk, got to run," I answered before racing out the front door.

I was halfway to the police station when I realized they would see me coming. That would ruin the whole point of having camouflage. I ducked down a nearby alley out of sight and whispered, "Go ahead" to Beau.

I felt Beau's magic cascade down my body, covering me in a soothing warmth. To anyone around us, we would appear invisible. Luckily, the front doors to the station opened of their own accord, letting me in without betraying my existence. The bullpen area was empty which wasn't unusual. Vinnie would either be in with the chief as they questioned Piper or off chasing down some clues at the hospital with Janice.

I left the bullpen behind, passed the single holding cell, and continued back to the short hall that boasted the station's single interview room. I stopped at the window and held my breath. Piper sat facing me. Chief Hayes sat opposite her with a notepad and pen on the table between them. A slim manila folder sat off to one side.

"I really don't know what else I can tell you. I was in the lighting booth when Janice collapsed," Piper insisted.

"We had the lab rush results on the items that Janice touched, and your fingerprints were found on the prop sword she was holding on stage when she collapsed."

"Well, yeah of course they were. The prop guys asked me to fix it before intermission ended."

"So, you admit you handled the item."

"There were other people around too. Wait, you think I did something to Janice?"

"From what I understand, you were her understudy. With her incapacitated, the lead role is yours now."

"Technically that's true, but I wouldn't hurt anyone."

"How would you describe your relationship with Janice?"

"I mean, sure, we aren't best friends … and she could be pretentious, but I would never make her sick just to get a part."

"I've heard that there was some animosity between the two of you about the fact she got the role over you."

"It hurts to be told you're not quite good enough at something. But I'm telling you, I wouldn't hurt her. That's childish."

"Can you think of anyone who might have wanted to hurt her?"

Piper's mouth hung open as she considered the question. I wanted to know the answer as much as Chief Hayes. I also wanted to believe Piper when she said she couldn't have done this to Janice. I'd made assumptions about people in the past when I'd been wrapped up in cases and it had turned out I was wrong. I didn't want to make the same mistake again.

"I mean, she kind of annoyed everyone on the crew." Piper leaned in closer, drawing the chief's attention. "We are a small troupe. This was our first big tour and she acted like we were about to be showcased on Broadway. She has an overinflated sense of herself sometimes, which I guess is what makes her a good actress."

"So, no one specific you can think of then?"

Piper's face fell. "No."

"You stated you worked in the lighting department, is that right?"

"Yes."

"Then why were you called to fix the prop?"

"I already told you; the prop boys are about as subtle as a bull in a china shop. They're always breaking things and I'm one of the only women on the crew. So, they think I'm supposed to be able to fix everything."

"And as far as you could tell, when you handled the prop sword, there was nothing unusual about it except that it needed to be fixed?"

"Nothing else out of the ordinary." Piper's brow furrowed. "Wait, no."

"Which is it, Miss Hennessey? Yes, there was something unusual or no, there wasn't?" Chief Hayes pressed.

"Not the sword exactly. I remember walking away after I'd fixed it, feeling kind of anxious. My heart was racing." Tears sparkled in her eyes as a few slipped past her lashes to dribble down her cheeks. "I know how that sounds, but I swear I didn't do anything to her. You can ask her."

On that note, Chief Hayes reached into his pocket and pulled out a cell phone. I could see Vinnie's name flashing on the screen. Without a word, he left the interview room and occupied the hallway.

As I'd done before, I pressed myself as close to the wall as possible. Even still, I could swear the chief's gaze moved over me as he answered the call.

"Give me some good news, Vinnie." For a split second I caught a glimmer of hope in the man's eyes. It died instantly. "I was afraid of that."

How I wished I could be privy to the other side of that conversation.

"They've gotten the tests back and you're sure ...?" Another pause as Vinnie answered the question on the other end of the phone. "Right. Well, you better head over and make sure everything is still secure."

Chief Hayes ended the call and pinched the bridge of his nose. I'd never seen him this worn down before. A small part of me appreciated that it made him feel more human.

After taking a few breaths, he dialed another number on his phone, holding it to his ear. "I'm going to need a lab technician to come to the station for a swab."

Ending the second call, he pocketed his phone and returned to the interview room.

"Can I go now?" Piper asked, sounding emotionally drained.

"We're not finished." The chief's voice took on a hard edge. "That call was from the hospital. Janice died twenty minutes ago due to severe anaphylaxis to peanuts."

"What? No, that can't be right. She can't be *dead*."

"That's what happens when you poison someone."

"But I didn't," Piper whined, her voice sliding up in pitch. "I swear to you I didn't."

"Well, we're going to find out. You're not going anywhere until the lab tech swabs your hands for any residue. And we'll be checking your room at the B&B as well."

Tania wouldn't appreciate the sudden encroachment in her space, but leaving to go warn her meant I'd miss whatever else Chief Hayes might get out of Piper. I stayed pressed against the window, the familiar weight of Beau's tiny claws on my shoulder.

"If there is anything else you want to tell me, now's the time," Chief Hayes' demeanor continued to intensify.

Piper shook in her seat on the opposite side of the interview room. I had to fight every urge within me to keep from bursting through the door to comfort her. Somehow, she managed to compose herself enough to dry her eyes with the backs of her hands and sat up.

"Well, uh ... there might be someone who might have wanted to hurt her," she finally offered.

"Not five minutes ago, you told me there was no one on the crew you thought would want to harm Janice."

"This isn't someone on the crew or in the cast."

I didn't need to see the chief's face to sense his outright irritation as he spoke. "Then who?"

"Janice had a stalker. At the start of the year, we did a few open rehearsals where people could come and watch before we started the tour. There was this guy, Levi, who came to every single rehearsal we did. He definitely gave off creepy vibes. The guy kept trying to get Janice to give him an autograph. I think he finally did too, mainly because she thought it would make him go away."

"This Levi have a last name?"

Piper hung her head. "I don't know it. But I think she'd been talking with the director to try and find a way to get some sort of harassment prevention order against him. Especially since he kept showing up on the tour."

"The director, Celia Voss?"

"Yeah, that's her."

"Did Levi know about her allergy?"

"I would bet my life on it," Piper answered.

"Can you describe him?"

Piper scratched at the nape of her neck for a moment. "Pretty tall. Like five-foot-eight, or maybe nine. He's got dark hair and this really intense stare."

"Eye color? Ethnicity?"

"I think his eyes are green. Maybe brown. I don't know, he creeped me out, too. I tried to avoid interacting with him as much as I could."

"You think his obsession would be enough to push him to kill her?"

"I wouldn't be surprised if he did. He's also kind of a Romeo and Juliet freak. Like he kept correcting other members of the cast when they flubbed lines."

"Have you seen him in town here?"

Her brow furrowed and she shook her head slowly. "I don't think so. But I wasn't really focused on Janice's drama. I had other things going on."

"Such as?"

My face heated and it had nothing to do with Beau's magical camouflage. So far, I'd managed to stay off the chief's radar. But if Piper was about to disclose our familial connection, that laser focus of his could be turned on me. Not that I had any relevant information to offer.

"Well, it turns out I've got some family in the area. A cousin two times removed, I think. We only just connected a couple days ago online, and we met for coffee yesterday."

"What's this cousin's name?"

"Darcy Ingram."

I expected him to react to my name, but his body language betrayed no emotion. "She was present last night during the show."

"Yeah. I gave her tickets. Well, my mom did. But the tour gives us a few free tickets for each show to hand out if we want. I think they want to try and make sure the theater is filled. Anyway, I thought it would be nice for her to come and see what I do. You know, a way for us to start to get to know each other. But she really wouldn't know anything about Janice or who'd want to hurt her."

"Let me worry about who knows what."

I heard the front doors slide open and heavy

footfalls signaled the arrival of the lab tech. A scrawny man with a mop of red curls and pale freckled cheeks traipsed past me, oblivious to my spying. He stopped at the interview room door and failed to stifle a yawn before he knocked twice. I caught Chief Hayes' body turn toward the sound and call, "Come in."

I watched as the tech donned latex gloves and rubbed swabs all over Piper's hands, securing each sample in its own clear evidence baggy before stowing them in his kit. As he turned toward the door I caught the bags under his eyes, too. Had everyone in law enforcement in this town been working all night?

"Put a rush on those. We have a killer on the loose," the chief instructed.

"I'll do my best," the tech replied before leaving.

"I've answered your questions and let you test me for whatever it is you think you'll find. Can I please go now?"

"Until we know the results of those swabs, I'm afraid you're going to have to stay here."

"Am I under arrest?"

"Not yet. But the law allows me to hold you for forty-eight hours without charges. Come with me."

"I want a phone call," Piper insisted as he led her

down the short hall to the holding cell. She balked at stepping inside, but he gave her no other option.

He pulled the door shut, locking it from the outside before retreating to his office. I felt the coolness of Beau's magic starting to dissipate. Looking around I caught sight of my hazy reflection in the glass and barely managed not to panic.

"Hang on just a little longer, Beau. Please," I whispered just as the chief reentered my line of sight with a cordless phone. The chameleon's magic shimmered, and my reflection disappeared again.

"You can make one call."

Please don't call me.

I realized as soon as the thought entered my head that she didn't have my mobile number as far as I was aware. So, there was very little likelihood she'd phone me. Though I wanted to give her some sort of sign that I knew what was happening and I would do all I could to prove she hadn't murdered Janice to get a role. But that would mean revealing myself to Chief Hayes. *That* would more than likely land me right there in the cell beside my cousin.

I stayed long enough to hear Piper say, "Mom" before the chief stepped away to give her privacy. I hurried through the bullpen, doing my best to time my exit with the Chief's opening and closing of his office door. Examining the sword Janice had touched might give me clues to how she'd been poisoned, but I'd already risked staying in the station too long. Moreover, given the brief bit of Vinnie and the chief's conversation I'd overheard, the hospital or lab likely still had the sword if they'd been testing it for evidence of substances like peanut residue. Finding another lead to give Chief Hayes was the best way to help Piper now.

There had to be clues at the theater that Chief Hayes and Vinnie missed—or didn't know to look for at the time. Maybe Janice had left some evidence that would show me where to find this stalker. Either way, I wasn't about to go snooping solo. I'd promised Maggie I would check in on her today and that was exactly what I intended to do. Besides, solving a mystery was pretty par for the course in our relationship.

8

Beau dropped his invisibility magic the moment we were out of sight of the police station and down a side street. I glanced down at the reptile and while most chameleons aren't that expressive, I could see the fatigue in his eyes. I stroked the top of his head and he leaned into the gesture.

"Sorry that took so long," I apologized as I made my way down Main Street toward Maggie's apartment. The sun glinted off the nearby windows as I walked, revealing empty storefronts. Not an unusual sight for a Sunday morning.

I reached Maggie's building a minute later and rang the bell for her second-floor unit. I waited for the door to buzz and unlock to allow me entry.

Except nothing happened. I tried the bell again and still no response. I pulled my phone from my pocket and dialed her number.

"Hi, you've reached Maggie. I'm not available right now. Please leave a message," her voicemail answered after just one ring.

I didn't bother leaving a message. There was only one other place I think she'd be. I retraced my steps and turned before I got to the B&B. Instead, I headed past High Time, which sat locked up tight, its neon sign dimmed, and continued to the town's clinic. Like many of the shops in town, it typically didn't boast Sunday morning hours. Yet, the lights were on inside and when I approached the front door, it slid open automatically.

"Maggie?" I called out as I walked inside.

My voice echoed in the space, bouncing off the shelves of neatly stocked medicinal products, many of Maggie's own recipes, along with mundane items like rubbing alcohol, iodine, and bandages. Still no reply came as I moved toward the back exam rooms and the office.

"Can you tell if she's here?" I whispered, addressing Beau.

'Back office. Worried.'

"Me, too." I approached the office to find the

door ajar. The sound of glass clinking drew my attention.

Not wanting to startle Maggie if she was in the middle of something, I made a point to clear my throat and knocked on the doorframe. "Maggie, you in here?"

The clinking stopped and Maggie peered around the edge of the door. She pulled off a set of wireless earphones. "Oh, sorry. I didn't hear you."

"Didn't mean to interrupt, but I did say I'd come by today to check on you. And you weren't at home."

Maggie's cheeks turned a shade of pink that made her red hair even more vibrant. She opened the door and allowed me to enter. I noticed a set of small vials filled with various colored liquids laid out on the desk. A larger container held a mixed purple concoction.

"Uh, I might have lied this morning when I said I was doing better," Maggie admitted, hanging her head.

Beau scurried down my left arm to settle on the desk between us, his tail winding around Maggie's pinkie finger. I closed the distance and lifted her chin, so our gazes met. "Tell us what's going on."

"I think whatever magic I sensed last night got in my head." She gestured toward the vials on the desk.

"I was trying to come up with something to help me feel less anxious, but whatever it was must still be affecting me."

"I'm starting to think that there is something more going on here," I said and moved to lean on the desk beside her. "Piper told Chief Hayes that she got this sort of anxious feeling when she was fixing the prop. Like she was scared."

"That's what I felt, too."

"I wish we could get a look at that sword, but it's still in police custody."

"You're not breaking into the police evidence locker," Maggie said sternly.

"I know. Besides, it's not technically there."

Maggie pinched the bridge of her nose. "I shouldn't ask how you know that. Or how you know what your cousin told Rick either."

"Well, then I definitely shouldn't tell you that Beau and I might have spied on them at the station."

"So much for not getting involved," she said.

I wanted to tell her I'd tried to stay out of it, but deep down, I knew that was a lie. The moment any suspicion fell on Piper, I'd been working to ensure she was protected. Apparently familial ties, even for those I'd just met, were stronger than I'd expected.

"She's being held at the station. I watched him lock her up."

"On what charges? Assault?"

"Actually, looks like murder. Janice is dead."

"Oh, God …"

"They said she had a severe allergic reaction. But you didn't notice anything that might have smelled like peanuts on her, did you?"

"Not that I remember."

"You were trying to do CPR. Would you have tasted it if she'd eaten it?"

"I didn't see anything like peanut oil on her hands."

"That's why Chief Hayes is holding Piper. They swabbed her hands to see if they've got residue on them."

"Well, if you can't examine the prop, what are you thinking of doing?"

"She mentioned that Janice had a stalker. Some bloke called Levi. Showed up at their open rehearsals before the tour and has been coming to every show. I doubt Chief Hayes was looking for signs of magic at the scene. Maybe we'd spot something that might give an explanation of how someone could have poisoned Janice."

"It feels a little risky, Darcy. Entering a crime scene?"

"Until a few minutes ago, it wasn't a crime scene. If we could get in before they lock it down and are careful, no one will ever know we were there. Please, Maggie, I need to see if there's anything at the theater that can help clear Piper's name."

"I didn't say I wasn't going to help," she answered, leaning over to pull open the top desk drawer and produced two pairs of medical gloves.

"Let's go."

MAGGIE LED the way out of the clinic and down an alley that took us to the rear of the theater. She'd already donned her gloves when she jiggled the lock on the back door. I heard something click and it swung outward on silent hinges.

"Why do you know how to break in here?" I hissed.

"I may have helped out with a few summer productions and this door has always been a little sticky. I wouldn't be surprised if someone with a little power made it not lock all the way, so they could sneak out for a smoke unnoticed," she answered.

The backstage area of the theater was cramped and dimly lit. It was a wonder there was any space at all for actors to change and get ready for their scenes back here. Not to mention the technical crew moving sets. Costumes hung haphazardly off rolling racks shoved to one side and a door marked 'Private' had light filtering beneath the frame.

"Is it always this cluttered?"

"Usually, the productions aren't as big or involved," Maggie answered and gestured to the sign on the door. "I would guess this was designated as Janice's dressing room. If they're trying to be even semi-professional, the leads would get their own changing space."

I looked around for any hint of where Romeo might have been sent to change, but this was the only door in sight. "I suppose the leads must have changed together?"

"Guess we'll find out," she replied and took a step toward the door.

I pulled on my gloves, grimacing at the chalky texture of the latex against my skin. I could feel my hands begin to dry out immediately. I reached the door first and turned the knob, forcing the door to open inward.

My guess as to whether the leads had shared a dressing room were confirmed by the dresses slung over the back of one chair while long pants and a ruffled shirt were strewn over the small sofa to my right. At first it looked like any dressing room would in the midst of an active production. I noted the distinct lack of items being rifled through, which suggested the police had not yet checked here.

"We might just get lucky," I muttered to myself as I approached the small vanity.

Easing the single central drawer open, I studied its contents. There was an EpiPen along with a cell phone that I suspected belonged to Janice. The pen looked unused. If she'd had any sort of reaction during intermission, she'd have likely used the medication before returning to the stage.

"Darcy, look at this," Maggie called as she bent over a trash bin.

I closed the drawer and joined her on the other side of the room. A bouquet of roses sat discarded, the delicate flowers smashed and crumpled against the wire frame of the bin. My heart ached at the sight of them. Not that roses held more meaning to me than any other flower, but at the sad state of them.

"I think there's a card," Maggie said and rummaged beneath the stems and leaves to pull out a small, folded card with Janice's name on the front. She turned it over and I read the message inscribed on it:

For the only true star of the show.

Knowing very little about Levi, I had no doubt this had come from him. It would explain why Janice had thrown the bouquet away. But did that mean he was in fact in town? I fought to free one hand of the glove, earning side eye from Maggie.

"I have an idea, but it needs direct physical contact," I explained.

This past fall, I'd learned I could sort of see through the metaphorical eyes of plants. It was like sometimes a psychic impression was left within them for me to pick up on. It wasn't foolproof, but I was hoping it would work this time. Maybe I could at least get a sense of who the flowers came from.

I sat on the edge of the seat in front of the vanity and held the stems of the bouquet in my ungloved hand. Closing my eyes, I focused my attention on the seeds of power within me. It still amazed me the ease with which I could call upon my magic now that I'd been able to nurture it. Power snapped to attention inside me, and I felt the flowers trying to respond to my touch. Though cut flowers had never been something I'd tried to use before in this way. I'd had a discarded piece of a larger whole once. However, it could only show me where it had been, not anything about the individual who'd severed it from the vine it originated from.

"Come on, I know you've had a rough go of it," I coaxed, using a soothing tone. "But I need to see how you ended up this way."

I felt Maggie's bare hand wrap around mine and warmth spread across my skin, adding her magic to my own. It was enough of a boost for the petals to perk up and I could feel something akin to a heartbeat pulsating against my fingertips.

When I opened my eyes again, Maggie had vanished, and my vision tinted pink to match the flowers' hue. Seeing through a plant's memories was always disorienting at first and I took a few deep breaths to steady myself. The bouquet had sat on the vanity as the door opened and Janice walked in followed by a young woman with bottle blonde hair.

"I thought you said you were going to take care of this," Janice spat, jabbing her finger angrily at the roses. "He's doing it again, Celia."

"He'll lose interest. And honestly, he hasn't done anything threatening."

"He's harassing me. Always shows up and sends me flowers. It's creepy and seriously ruining my creative process."

"You've got a fan, Janice. I thought you'd be happy."

"I would be happy if I never saw him again. I swear, he's unstable." She knocked the bouquet into the bin and pulled out her phone. "Look, he's been sending me messages, too. I have my number unlisted and somehow, he got my private cell phone. And he's stalking me online, too." She tapped the screen, revealing a profile page for a Levi Sanders.

"Okay, okay, I get it. When this set of shows is over, we'll figure out how to get a restraining order. For now, just focus on the rest of the show tonight."

Janice waved Celia away and turned to study her reflection in the mirror, trying to smooth out worry lines around her lips. I watched her apply moisturizer to her face and wipe the excess off with a towel. Nothing indicated she was about to have an allergic reaction. I did manage to catch a glimpse of her costume. It appeared to be what she had worn in the act when she collapsed.

A few moments later, someone knocked at the

door and a male voice called, "Janice, we need you back on stage. Curtain is about to go up."

Janice reapplied her lipstick, glanced in the mirror one last time and answered, "Coming, Benji."

The room around me went dark as the spell faded. I blinked a few times to clear my vision and set the flowers back in the bin.

"It looks like these might have come from her stalker."

"That's not good."

"No, and it looks like they showed up partway through the show, which suggests he could have been in the theater."

"Was she exposed to anything?"

"Just some face lotion," I answered and spotted the container sitting on the vanity surface. I picked it up with my gloved hand and sniffed. A soothing mix of lavender and cucumber. No hint of peanuts anywhere.

"That doesn't mean he couldn't have somehow messed with the props when he was delivering the flowers," Maggie noted.

"Or he had someone on the inside helping him. We need to see what we can find out about this guy, Levi Sanders. I saw his full name on Janice's phone."

"Where to then?"

We need to head back to Tania's. I think we should talk to the director and get her take on how dangerous this guy really was."

'Leave now.'

Beau's warning caught me off guard. He'd been riding on Maggie's shoulder, and he'd blended into her shirt's fabric so completely I'd forgotten he was with us. A moment later I picked up on the sound of a distant door opening. Maggie and I left the dressing room, careful to pull the door shut just as we'd found it and retreated through the back door just in time to avoid being caught.

9

The B&B was buzzing with activity when Maggie and I walked through the front door. We could hear a dozen conversations filtering through the first floor and the clatter of dishes on the counter in the kitchen. I followed the cacophony to find Tania flitting about the space, setting dishes in the sink to soak while refilling a carafe of coffee.

"What did we miss?" I asked.

Tania spun, empty coffee pot in one hand. "Oh, Vinnie came by to search through Piper's things."

Digging into Levi flitted to the back of my mind. "Where is Audrey?"

"She left with Vinnie. Probably to go down to the station to see Piper."

"Do you know if Vinnie found anything?"

Tania shook her head. "Sorry. I stayed out of the way. But the poor thing looked exhausted when he left. "

"Can I help with the guests?" I held my hands out to take the carafe of coffee.

Tania looked at Maggie before inclining her head towards me. "I see she's pulled you into this mess."

"Oi, I'm standing right here. And can you blame me for wanting to prove Piper's innocence?"

"Not twelve hours ago, you agreed that you didn't know her well enough to judge her culpability."

"I remember. But I also have to believe that Nan put her in my path for a reason and it wasn't to ruin another familial connection." I plucked the carafe from her hands. "I'm going to see who needs a refill."

I left Maggie and Tania in the kitchen, and wound my way through the dining room. I spotted some of the background actors sitting around one end of the dining table and stopped to offer them a top up.

"Do you have anything stronger?" an Asian woman with an elaborate braid asked.

"Afraid not, sorry."

"I hate small towns," she muttered and turned back to looking at her phone.

The man sitting beside her gestured to his empty mug. "Ignore her. She doesn't handle stress well."

"I'm not judging. I can't imagine the upheaval you all must be feeling now. Will they even continue the shows?"

"Hard to do Romeo and Juliet without Juliet," Lucy interjected.

She had a point. And with Piper currently in custody, that left them without a lead of any sort. But they likely didn't know that yet. "Did you not have back-ups?" I feigned ignorance.

"Oh, we've got an understudy, but she's gone MIA," the man answered.

"She's not MIA. She's probably hiding, because everyone knows she was mad Janice was in the spotlight all the time," Lucy griped.

I didn't need to be an empath to sense the hostility towards my cousin. "You don't really believe one of your own crew would do something like that, would you?"

"Sitting up there, plotting and planning? Of course, she could do it," Lucy answered.

"If you want to know what she was really thinking, talk to Benji. They worked together twenty-four seven," the man said in a neutral tone and gestured in the direction of the living room.

That was the second time the name Benji had come up this morning. First, I'd heard him at the door to the dressing room in my flower-induced vision and now I was being directed to speak with him by a troupe member. It was worth following up, but I still needed to know who might have facilitated Levi's entry into the theater to leave the flowers for Janice last night.

"Thanks." I set the carafe down on the table. "Actually, do you know where I might find Celia, the director?"

"She's been upstairs in her room all morning. I think she's trying to figure out how much money we're going to lose if we have to cancel the rest of the tour," Lucy offered.

"God, could you be any more of a buzzkill, Luce?"

Thankfully, Tania kept a logbook by the stairs that denoted each guest and their room number. I did a lap through the living room, catching Benji sitting alone in the corner as I made my way back to the front of the house. After confirming Celia was in Room 1, I darted up the stairs to the second floor. The door to Room 1 sat closed and I stopped. I'd had an excuse to talk to some of the other cast and crew downstairs. No such reason existed now.

I raised my hand to knock just as the door flew open and Celia stepped across the threshold. I lowered my hand before I smacked her in the face. Her eyes were red rimmed which suggested she'd been crying. Had she become privy to the news that Janice hadn't made it?

"Can I help you?" Her voice was hoarse, which lent further credence to her emotional state.

"Sorry, I'm Darcy. I live here and have been helping Tania out. I just wanted to come check on you and see if you needed anything."

"What I need I don't think anyone can give me," she retorted. After a beat, she let out a long breath. "Sorry, I get a bit snippy when I'm stressed out."

"I'd be worried if you weren't stressed out given what's happened."

"I still don't understand how it could have happened," she sighed.

I gestured to the top stair riser and together we sat shoulder to shoulder. "How do you mean?"

"I made sure that there were absolutely no peanuts, no peanut oil anywhere in any of the theaters we went to on this tour. Everyone on the crew knew to avoid it. And yet, the police just told me that she died from a severe allergic reaction."

"Oh, I'm so sorry to hear she passed away."

"They think there might have been foul play."

"Oh, that's why they asked to talk to Piper this morning." If Celia thought I was as in the dark as her, she might be more willing to open up to me.

"Piper is a nice girl. She's not mean-spirited. I know some people think she was bitter about the fact she didn't get the lead role, but admittedly Janice is … I mean was the better actress."

"I haven't known Piper long, but she doesn't seem the type to do something like this."

Celia went quiet, her jaw working to put whatever was on her mind into words.

"I was just downstairs, and I heard from some people that there was someone who'd been following Janice from show to show?"

"Yeah, Levi."

"Maybe he sent her a gift not knowing it could hurt her?"

Celia shook her head. "Oh, he knew everything about her. All you had to do was look at his social media." She made a scoffing sound. "I feel like part of this is my fault. She kept telling me he freaked her out. That he made her feel unsafe and I didn't do anything."

"I'm sure that isn't true." Levi looked like a better suspect by the second.

"I put off doing anything about it, because I thought it was too complicated. And now he might have actually done something I could have stopped. Ugh, I have to tell her parents. I don't know how I'm going to do that."

"I'm sure the police will do all that. I've been around a few investigations since I moved here and they're good at getting to the truth." Or at least arresting the proper culprit in the end, even if they don't know about the supernatural happenings going on in the background.

"Thank you for listening," Celia said, grabbing my wrist as I tried to stand.

"Happy to do what I can." I got to my feet.

She released her grip on me and I descended the stairs to the first floor, intent on finding Benji. The corner he'd occupied earlier was now vacant. I did a slow lap of the first floor, but he was nowhere to be seen.

"You look like a witch on a mission," Sam's voice called from the direction of the back door.

Not wanting to draw unnecessary attention to myself in front of our grieving guests, I stepped outside, easing the door shut behind me. Sam floated by the fence that separated Tania's property from the one next door.

"There's this bloke called Benji who I think might have some information that could help Piper."

"Remind me again why you're so keen to help some stranger who might have just offed the competition?" I glared at him, and he shrugged one rhinestone studded shoulder back at me. "A ghost hears things."

"Because she's family and I honestly don't think she did it. Not when there's a perfectly viable suspect in this stalker the victim was fending off."

"So, why talk to the emo lighting guy? Unless you think he's involved?"

"He might be able to provide me with more context that could help clear Piper of any wrongdoing. And for all I know, he might know something about the stalker, too."

Sam arched a brow. "Well, I won't lie, if you want to know the dirt on what's happening in a theater troupe, it is always the backstage folks who know what's happening. People always seem to forget they exist."

"I'm sensing some unresolved issues there," I noted.

"Well, talking to him is going to be difficult seeing as he took off about ten minutes ago."

Bugger.

"Where'd he go?"

"How should I know? I'm here talking to you."

"A fat lot of good you are then," I muttered.

"He couldn't have gone far. And besides, he'll be back. It isn't like he actually knows anyone in town."

Sam wasn't wrong. It wasn't like I could do anything to get Piper released faster. Chief Hayes would hold her until he got the results of the swabs. My deep dive into Levi would have to be my next step.

I left Sam in the backyard and retreated to the kitchen. Tania had gone off to tend to the guests and Maggie remained, washing the dishes.

"You don't have to do that you know," I pointed out.

"I needed something to occupy my hands. And Tania looked like she could use the help. Find out anything useful?"

"Celia is pretty convinced that Levi had something to do with Janice's death. Which is good news for Piper."

"Assuming no evidence turns up that actually links her to the crime."

"I wanted to talk to Benji, the lighting guy since I'd heard him in my plant vision. But he's gone off somewhere. That leaves seeing what we can find out ourselves online about Levi."

Putting his name into a search yielded multiple social media profiles. I clicked on the top result to find his Facebook page restricted. All I could glean from it was he was originally from somewhere in Maine and he was born on the 5th of October. I didn't know how many Levi Sanders there were in the U.S., but the photograph attached to the profile matched Piper's description. Even though, it was decidedly unhelpful information.

I navigated back to the search results and selected his Instagram page. That social media profile, however, was a gold mine. Albeit a disturbing, gold mine. Scrolling back for at least the past two months revealed him taking selfies along the troupe's tour. There were even candid shots of Janice on stage.

"Celia wasn't kidding when she said he knew everything about her," I whispered, showing Maggie one of the posts where Levi had gone overly poetic about Janice and how she'd gotten her start in local theater as a child.

"Does he say anything about knowing she was allergic to peanuts?"

I skimmed past some more posts, but nothing

obvious came up. "No, but if he knew what childhood theater productions she was in, I doubt he wouldn't know that about her." I checked a few more of the posts. "He's been tagging her in all of his posts, too. No wonder she felt like he was constantly harassing her."

"People with obsessions like this can turn violent," Maggie said, shutting off the water and drying her hands on a dish rag.

It was a sad truth and one I suspected might have played out here. It didn't explain the strange sense of anxiety both Maggie and Piper had felt, or the odd bits of magic Maggie had detected. But then, if Piper had tried her best to avoid Levi, it was possible she wasn't aware he possessed magic. He wouldn't be the first person to hide his skills and use them to get what he wanted. Almost six months ago, Andrew Webster had been murdered by his own daughter who'd concealed her own magic to do the deed.

"Celia wasn't sure if Levi was in town for yesterday's show. But you can tag locations on these kinds of posts, right?"

Maggie nodded. "Not everyone does, but if you tap the image, it should give that information."

I checked a few of the older posts from the start of the tour. They showed locations throughout the

Northeast, getting closer to Brookhaven as they went along. The most recent post was from yesterday with a photo outside the theater. The post simply read, 'Ready to surprise my leading lady.' I spotted the bouquet of roses in his arms. Well, that gave a definitive answer as to whether he'd made it to town and could have been involved in her death. I tapped the image to find he hadn't tagged the location. For the moment, I wasn't interested in where or when he'd posted the image from. Something far more interesting had caught my attention. I enlarged the image and turned the phone toward Maggie.

"Tell me what you see."

Maggie studied the picture, sliding her finger across the screen to get a better view of the whole image. She slid the image up to reveal his hand holding the bouquet. "He's got gloves on."

"That's what I thought I noticed too." Temperatures had been cool by my standards all month, but he wasn't even wearing a jacket in the photo. But no one else had been wearing gloves in this weather.

Something felt very off about the whole thing. I closed the photo so I could double check the time he posted and see if he'd left any location data. The post went up about twenty minutes before Janice collapsed and the authorities were called. Plenty of time for him to have used magic to coat the prop sword in peanut oil. He could have even gotten it stuck so that Piper would have had to fix it, giving the police another suspect.

Still, there was something not quite right about the whole situation. I couldn't put my finger on what though. I'd gotten the impression Chief Hayes didn't entirely believe Piper when she told him about Levi. I stowed my phone and started for the front door when it opened from the outside to reveal Piper and Audrey standing on the threshold. Without thinking, I threw my arms around my cousin.

"They let you go."

She pulled back. "How'd you know they held me?"

"It doesn't matter. They released you, which means they must not think you're a person of interest anymore."

"They said the evidence was inconclusive. But they didn't have anything else, so they let me go."

It wasn't the exoneration I was hoping for, but it was a step in the right direction. And with Piper no longer stuck behind bars, we might have a chance to uncover the true culprit.

10

I got Piper settled in the kitchen with a cup of Maggie's special blend of chamomile tea. I could almost swear her hands were hot even before I passed her the mug. She grasped the teacup so tight that it turned her knuckles white. And I could see tension tightening her shoulders. But we still didn't know each other well enough for me to say anything. Just as I'd set the kettle back on the stove, news broke throughout the rest of the B&B that Janice wasn't merely convalescing in hospital, but that she'd died. Maggie had gotten a call about an emergency at the clinic and had taken off, leaving me and Tania to corral the guests.

"I can't believe they let you come back," Lucy said upon spotting Piper sitting beside me.

"I know I'm not an American, but I'm pretty sure you lot still have a system of innocent until proven guilty," I quipped.

"Lucy's just jealous she got relegated to ensemble," a vaguely familiar voice said from the far end of the kitchen.

I turned to see Benji standing there. Giving him a quick once over revealed nothing about where he might have gone. Not until he set down a travel cup with Ginny's name emblazoned across the center.

"That's rich, coming from the guy who can't even set foot on the stage," Lucy argued back.

"Can we not?" Piper shouted. "Janice is dead. You can think I did it if you want, I get you need someone to blame. But if any of you bothered to pay attention, you'd have seen I was perfectly happy behind the scenes."

"Besides, when exactly could Piper have done anything to her?" Benji interjected, jumping to my cousin's defense.

"I saw her fixing the prop right before intermission," Lucy retorted.

"That's enough out of all of you," Celia's voice rang out. She appeared from the dining room, putting herself between Piper and Lucy. "We are supposed to be adults, so stop squabbling like children. I've cleared it with the police that we can hold a small vigil for Janice outside the theater tomorrow night. So, let's focus on making it something worthy of our leading lady."

Celia made a point to physically move Lucy in the other direction, leaving Piper, Benji, and I in the kitchen. Benji moved to sit on Piper's other side. "I'm sorry you had to listen to all of that."

"I'd be surprised if she didn't have something nasty to say to me."

"Why is that?" I interrupted.

"Lucy worshipped the ground Janice walked on," Piper answered.

"If anyone knows what happened, it's her. I bet that's why she's so defensive," Benji added.

"Did you notice anything strange that night?" I addressed my question to him.

"Me? Like what?"

"I don't know. I was talking to Celia earlier and she mentioned something about there being some bloke that might have been following Janice around?" I would explain my snooping to Piper in private. Benji didn't need to know about mine or Beau's magical abilities.

"Levi. Yeah, he was a creep. I told the police they should be looking into him," Piper added.

"I don't think I saw him, but I didn't leave the lighting booth until the police showed up," Benji answered.

That was a lie.

"You must have," Piper contradicted. "You weren't there when I got back up after I fixed the sword."

"I meant, I didn't see Janice. I was in the bathroom."

Piper fixed him with a disbelieving look, but said nothing more. Silence fell over the space, and she turned her attention to finishing her cup of tea. I looked around, realizing Audrey had vanished.

"Where's your mum?"

"Probably off trying to find me a lawyer. She's terrified I'm going to be arrested."

"I would say them letting you leave after being questioned is a good sign," I reminded her.

"Mom said they tossed our room, but it didn't look like they found much," Piper replied.

"You should make sure they didn't ruin any of the costumes," Benji urged.

"Why don't I help you sort through whatever Vinnie did," I offered.

Piper nodded her agreement and I let her take the lead up the stairs. I expected to find Audrey in the room, but she must have taken her lawyer hunt elsewhere. The way Benji had described the situation, I feared the room would be a disaster.

"It's not so bad," I said. There were some clothes moved around on the beds and the closet door sat open, but nothing looked ruined.

"I still can't believe this is all happening," Piper sighed.

"I didn't exactly tell you the whole truth down there about Levi," I shared. "I heard you mention him."

Her brow furrowed in confusion. "When?"

"When you were talking to the chief at the police station."

"But you weren't there."

I sat down on the edge of the nearest bed and she joined me. "I'll let you in on a little secret. Since I moved here, I've ended up tangled in more than one mystery and I'm not the only one with magic around here. I've got a friend that can turn invisible and sometimes if he's feeling generous, he can hide me, too."

"You spied on the police for me?"

"I was worried. For me, family isn't exactly easy to come by and I didn't want to lose you right after I'd found you."

"Did Celia really tell you about Levi, though?"

"She did. She's afraid the fact she didn't do anything before might have let him get close to Janice to try and hurt her. I did a little light social media digging and he's clearly obsessed with her."

"It's horrible to say, but I honestly didn't understand why. She wasn't going to be famous," Piper said, studying her nails.

"I need to show you something," I said, retrieving my phone and pulling up Levi's most recent post, showing him carrying the flowers. "This was his last post. It was twenty minutes before she collapsed."

"So, he did manage to show up," she sighed.

"I found the flowers discarded in the rubbish bin in the dressing room. And this post proves he was there and brought them."

"You think the flowers could have had something on them? Like he doused them with peanut oil or something?"

"Could have. And look, he's wearing gloves. It's cool out, but not glove weather. What if he was trying to avoid leaving his fingerprints?"

"I bet he did try to kill her. He's not only obsessed with her, but with the play. I think he believes it would be romantic for them to both die together."

"We should post about the vigil Celia is putting together. If he was such a fan of Janice, I'm sure he couldn't help but show up. It would give the police an easy way to scoop him up," I proposed.

"It's not a bad idea. But shouldn't we tell the police what we're planning?"

"I would have thought you'd want to steer clear of the police station after this morning."

"I just want all of this to go away." She handed me the phone back. "The lady who owns the coffee shop, she knew the police were coming to bring me in."

"Ginny is Chief Hayes' sister. If I had to guess, she probably clued him in that you were there and that's how he found us."

"But why would she tell me to eat up?"

"Ginny's pretty clued into what's going on in town and I mean everything. I think it's part of her powers."

"She's got magic, too?"

"Yep. People around her tend to tell the truth."

Piper fixed me with a pointed look. "Is that why you suggested we go there for breakfast this morning? So, you could ask me questions and I'd have had to tell the truth?"

I hung my head. "Maybe a little."

"Part of me wants to be mad, but it's a sound strategy." After a pause she added, "Do you think we could convince her to come to the vigil? Maybe even get her to make Levi confess?"

"It's certainly worth asking."

One thing was still not adding up for me. "When I was at the theater earlier, I didn't pick up on anything strange about the flowers."

"You broke into a crime scene?"

"Technically it hadn't been declared a crime scene yet."

"How could you tell if there was magic?"

"It wouldn't have been the first time I was doused with magic-laced floral arrangements. But they seemed normal."

"Well, maybe the magic got used up when Janice collapsed."

It was as valid an assumption as anything I'd put forward. I wish I knew more about magic in general. "I think I might have an idea who we can ask about putting spells on everyday objects," I said, pulling Piper to her feet.

"What about telling the police about the photo Levi took? And the flowers?"

"We'll stop by there on our way. Come on."

I EXPECTED to find Chief Hayes in his office at the station, but it was empty. The bullpen was quiet, too, but I heard rummaging sounds from deeper in the space. I cleared my throat.

"Hello? Chief Hayes?"

A door closed and Vinnie appeared, looking strung out on too much caffeine to keep himself going. "The chief isn't here right now. Is there something I can help you with, Darcy?"

"I hope so." I pointed to Piper. "Well actually, I think it's Piper you ought to talk to. She's got some information you might find helpful in your investigation."

"I'm sure the chief told you about Levi, Janice's stalker," Piper began, taking out her own phone and pulling up Levi's profile online. "I found this post he made the other day and thought it seemed kind of suspicious."

Vinnie barely stifled a yawn as he looked at her phone. "You're concerned about a photo of a guy with flowers?"

I gestured for Piper to keep talking and mimed pulling on gloves. She double tapped the screen to enlarge the photo. "Look at this. He's wearing gloves. That's unusual. And he's got a history of stalking Janice. Everyone in the troupe knew about it."

"I'll take a report and add it to the file."

With Vinnie momentarily occupied, I slipped back to the hallway leading to the interview room and the evidence lock up. The door sat ajar, and I held my breath as I eased it open further. Vinnie had left the box of evidence open sitting on a shelf. I could see the prop sword in an plastic bag sticking out.

I didn't need to touch it to sense there was definitely something off about the object. A wave of anxiety crashed over me before I'd even tried to move the box's lid out of the way. For a split second, my magic sputtered within me, as if the seed of my power was withering by the second.

I backed out of the closet and eased the door shut again. The anxiety clung to me like stress sweat and I shivered as I returned to the bullpen. With any luck, our next stop would provide some much-needed answers.

"I know I don't really need to remind you, Miss Hennessey, but you can't leave town until this is all wrapped up," Vinnie said.

"I understand. Thank you for listening, Officer."

She stowed her phone. "And obviously, you know I'm at the B&B if you have any more questions."

I waited until we were half a block away from the station to exhale. The anxiety ebbed with more distance from the prop. "There is definitely something magical about that sword, but I don't understand it."

"You got that anxious feeling, too?"

"So, did Maggie when she was near it on stage."

"But why would it make us anxious and lead to Janice dying?"

"I have no idea. That's what we need to find out."

I led Piper to the edge of town to find a shop set away from the rest of the shops in Brookhaven. Tyson's Treasures was the only pawn shop in town. And it was protected by magic courtesy of Ginny Hayes herself. I'd encountered Tyson for the first time not long after I'd moved to town. Town gossip held that he'd been ripped off too many times. Now whenever anyone enters his shop, they can only speak the truth about what they've come to bargain for or sell. If anyone was going to know about why magical items affected people differently, it would be him.

"Are you sure this guy will help us? I mean it's not like we've got anything to offer to sell him."

"There's only one way to find out."

The bell above the door announced our presence in the cramped space. It looked unchanged from my last visit six months ago. Although a few of the items on display in the glass case had changed position and were accompanied by a few new pieces.

"Darcy Ingram," Tyson's voice echoed from the depths of the shop.

"Uh, hello."

The slender, dark-skinned proprietor appeared in profile before he moved to stare at me with such an intensity. It almost made me want to turn and run the other way. Somehow, I stood my ground.

"How does he know your name?" Piper stage whispered. She took a half-step back from the counter, as if his very presence unnerved her.

"Well, when you keep ending up entwined in the business of this town's inhabitants on a semi-frequent basis, it makes certain people sit up and take notice," Tyson answered.

"And that includes a pawn shop owner?" Piper arched a brow.

"I make it my business to know what's going on in this town. How else do you expect me to ensure the provenance of the items I acquire?"

"Didn't really think about it," Piper responded.

Tyson turned his focus back on me. "You're making something of a reputation for yourself around here."

"It's not by design, I promise."

He leaned on the counter, pointing a bony finger at me. "But you like it. Don't deny it."

I wasn't sure I could physically deny it, not while in Tyson's store. "You're right. I don't mean to get wrapped up in things, it just happens. But I can't deny that it's also given me the chance to improve my magic."

"Having another competent witch in this town isn't something I'll argue with." He stood up to his full height. "Why don't you tell me why you've come?"

"We need to know everything about how someone could spell a mundane item to kill an innocent person."

11

Tyson drummed his slender fingers along the countertop separating us for a moment before speaking. "I'm going to need more information than that."

"I don't know if you heard, but the lead in our production was murdered," Piper interjected.

"You must not be from a small town. News travels lightning quick around here. Although, I admit I wasn't aware the poor woman had died."

"They said she died from a severe reaction. She was deathly allergic to anything peanut," Piper explained.

"But from what we can gather, there wasn't anything around with peanuts on it. But she clearly had a reaction after touching a prop on stage."

"That seems to be your culprit, then."

"That's what we thought, but neither of us remember smelling anything like peanuts on the prop. And if it was enough to kill her, it had to be all over it," I added.

"And we both got this strange sense of anxiety when we were near it," Piper continued.

"Maggie, too. She was trying to give Janice first aid."

"It isn't impossible for magic to affect people differently, especially when one of those people isn't magical."

"I mean, Janice had thought she was God's gift to acting, but I'm pretty sure she wasn't a witch," Piper said.

"Make no mistake, I do not condone doing anything of the sort. But it is possible if you've got the right sort of magic to use an object holding some kind of significance to a person to reflect back something like their deepest fear. If you were not the intended target, you could suffer side effects from the spell."

"Like anxiety about my magic fading?" I blurted.

"Or outing me as a witch to everyone and catching everything on fire?" Piper added.

Or Maggie doubting her healing abilities?

"Yes. All possibilities. But I can assure you I have not sold anything that might help facilitate such an attack."

"We're pretty sure the person came from out of town," I replied, glancing in Piper's direction. "Would you say that prop sword had any special significance to Janice?"

"I mean, she was always fond of the death scene for some reason. She thought it was poignant."

"But you had to have other swords," I pressed.

She shook her head. "That was used specifically for that scene, and we only had the one. It's the reason why I had to keep fixing it."

"What sort of magic might be able to do this?" I focused back on Tyson. "More emotional magic, right?"

"Most likely. Someone who might be able to manipulate the perception of others."

Perception?

"Could magic trick someone into believing they were having such a severe reaction that their body shut down?"

"If the caster is powerful enough, magic can do a great many things."

It might explain why none of us could smell any peanut oil or any other byproducts anywhere on

Janice, the prop, or the flowers. She could have been compelled to believe it was there and so terrified of being poisoned that her mind tricked itself into believing it was happening.

"This has been really helpful, thank you," I told Tyson.

"I see that look in your eyes. You're off to hunt down this evil doer."

The magic within the shop compelled me to tell the truth. "I have an idea of how we might find them."

"You do?" Piper interjected.

"Well, I did. See, my magic can tap into plants, even ones that aren't strictly alive anymore."

"Like flowers that have been cut for a bouquet?"

"Exactly. I used my powers and the same technique to try following the trail of a different killer months back." It was how I'd first encountered Tyson.

"But that would mean getting the flowers from the theater."

"Except I don't think it's doable now. It might not have been a crime scene before, but it definitely is now."

"Have you forgotten where you are?" Tyson quipped. He set a small black metallic fob watch on the counter between us. "So long as your intent is clear, this can lead you as your own magic would."

"What do you want in return? I don't have anything of value to you," I replied, uneasy about such a bargain.

"You're turning into something of a respectable sleuth, Miss Ingram. I will give you this on the promise that you'll owe me one magical favor."

"We can find another way to track down Levi," Piper insisted.

I didn't like the thought of owing Tyson or anyone else anything. Besides, we already had the plan to lure Levi to the vigil tomorrow. But first we needed to find out what sort of magic he had, if only to prepare ourselves for another attack.

"Fine. I'll owe you one." I took the watch and marched out of the shop, Piper hot on my heels.

"You really didn't have to do that," she repeated as I power walked in the direction of the center of town.

"Luring him out is a good plan, but we still need to know what we're really up against," I explained.

"So, this thing takes us to him. What do we do if he sees us? He'll know me from the troupe."

I stopped mid-stride. Maybe I'd been too hasty in accepting Tyson's deal after all. It was a reasonable conclusion that Levi would be laying low after Janice's murder to avoid suspicion. And even if he'd geotagged his photo, it would probably only lead the police right back to the theater—a dead end.

I pivoted on my heel to face my cousin. "Have you got any better ideas, cousin?"

"Well, not everyone in the crew shunned me. A lot of the backstage guys, props notwithstanding, know a lot about what goes on. I think before we even attempt to hunt Levi down, we need to confirm his movements to the best of our ability by talking with the crew."

"Maybe this can still help us with that," I pushed.

"I know you want to find him. Believe me, I do, too. But we need to trust the people in the crew."

I pocketed the watch and let her take the lead back to the B&B as the sun started its afternoon descent. I realized as we approached the front steps that I'd skipped lunch entirely. With any luck, Tania would have a spread laid out buffet style in the dining room for dinner, which would give us decent cover to ask our questions.

As I'd hoped, the tantalizing scent of grilled chicken with rice and beans filled the air. I traced the familiar path to the dining room and picked up a plate. Piper slid into step beside me, indicating with a small jut of her chin to a pair of women in all black, their vibrant hair the only thing setting them apart from one another.

"That's Bree and Andrea, they handle costumes. They would have been around to help Janice get into her wardrobe for the rest of the play."

"They could have seen something," I murmured. "You think they'll talk to you about it?"

"Only one way to find out."

She moved out ahead of me down the table, using tongs to snap up a few slices of chicken, and ladle beans and rice onto her plate. I followed suit and we squeezed in to sit at the small card table Tania had set out beside where the two women stood.

"How are you holding up after Lucy's tirade, Piper?" one of the women asked. She sported hair the color of cotton candy.

"I'm okay, Bree, thanks," Piper answered.

That left the one with the shock of lime green braids to be Andrea. I took a few bites of food, hoping to make my question appear nonchalant. "Piper said you two do costumes for the tour?"

"We made most of them ourselves," Andrea boasted.

"Brilliant. They were really good."

Bree looked around, her face falling. "Oh, no … do you think they had to cut her out of her Juliet dress at the hospital?" She looked appalled at the thought.

"Piper's got her backup," Andrea reminded her. "Though I don't know if you'll get to use it."

"Let's worry about laying Janice to rest first," Piper answered. "I appreciate you two not automatically assuming it was me."

"Benji is right, you're not a vindictive bi—" Andrea began, but stopped herself from swearing. "But my money is on that psycho stalker."

"We were looking at Janice's social media and we saw he had tagged her in a photo yesterday. He was at the theater bringing her flowers," Piper said.

"That was him?" Bree's surprise appeared genuine.

"You saw him bring in the flowers?" I prodded.

"Well, not exactly. I was busy trying to get the background cast ready for after intermission. It's kind of a mad dash, especially in a small theater like the one here. They showed up right before intermission. I didn't think to look at who brought the flowers. I mean, we all know what he looks like, I guess I was just distracted."

"Do you remember if he was coming from the front of the theater or the back?" Piper asked.

"I think it must have been the back. I mean, the only way to get backstage from the front entrance is through the theater itself and it would have been pretty obvious to see a guy walking through with flowers."

It was entirely possible Levi had taken the photo at the front of the theater before sneaking around back. As Maggie had shown, it wasn't hard to gain entry through the rear exit. And it would have allowed him easier access to the dressing room. Although that would have meant he had prior knowledge of the space.

Bree and Andrea turned back to their meal, ending our discussion of Levi and the flowers. There were still other people we could ask about his movements. "Piper, you said you had to go fix a prop right before intermission ended, where was that?"

"We had a little props area set up on the other side of the stage. Why?"

"How did you get back there?"

"I went down the far aisle in the theater and up onto the stage."

"What about when you were coming back?"

"I ducked behind the curtain on the stage, behind the scenery."

"Could Levi have gone that way to avoid being seen after dropping off the flowers in the dressing room?"

"It's possible. I was only down there for a couple of minutes, but he might have come that way." The realization dawned on Piper, and she let out a groan. "Ugh! That means we have to actually talk to those jerks."

We didn't have to look far to find the props team. They were hanging in the backyard having a mock sword fight with foam weaponry. Piper assured me they hadn't taken it from the theater. They just brought them along, because they liked to pretend they were stunt choreographers and props masters.

"Hey look, it's the not-quite Juliet," one of them said.

"Danny, you're the definition of toxic masculinity," Piper quipped. "I need you to stop being idiots for a minute, because I have a question and it's really important."

One of the other guys laid down his foam sword and moved to wrap a beefy arm around Danny's shoulders. "What's up?"

"We've been hearing that Levi might have

slipped past the crew and gotten into the dressing room during the show last night."

"No way," Danny argued. "We'd have kicked his creeper ass out of there."

"We think he might have been posing as a delivery person," I interjected. "Could have walked right past you."

"No. All I saw was some old guy getting lost looking for the bathroom," Danny insisted.

"Thanks for nothing," Piper grumbled and slunk off around the front of the house to sit on the front steps. I wasn't so sure she needed to be that upset. I hurried to join her and pulled out my phone.

"They might have actually been on to something," I said.

"What are you talking about?"

I pulled up Levi's post again and zoomed in on the image. This time, instead of studying the flowers or the fact he was wearing gloves, I pointed to the edge of what looked to be a shoulder strap on a bag.

"We were so busy looking at the flowers that we missed this."

"It could be anything."

"What if Bree, Andrea, and Danny were all right. Or at least they thought they were." The words tumbled out of my mouth. "You said that Levi was into acting and that everyone knew what he looked like, right?"

"Yeah. Everyone had photos of him on their phone in case we spotted him. We hadn't been kicking him out of all the shows, but we were starting to since he kept trying to get in Janice's personal space after wrap."

"Then he'd have needed to get creative if he really wanted to keep seeing Janice in every performance. What if he brought disguises to fool people? If he'd been around since the start of the production, he would know that a lot of the backstage people would be busy during intermission, and he could sneak in."

"That's devious," Piper whispered.

"Or bloody brilliant. Because if the police asked, anyone who saw him would say they saw someone different. Like an old man or a delivery driver. If you think about it, it's actually genius."

"How far in advance would he have known the location of all the stops on the tour?"

"I think we put them out like three months ago. That's when we started pushing sales to make sure we could cover travel—hotels and everything. You think he scoped this place out?"

"If he was truly dedicated to Janice and knew you

were closing ranks on him, he had to be smart enough to cover his tracks.”

“Is it possible he could use magic to disguise himself?”

“Anything’s possible,” I answered.

We now had a sense of the path he might have taken to leave the flowers. It could have given him close enough proximity to do something to the prop sword with time to sneak out the back again while everyone was distracted by Janice’s collapse on stage.

“We have an idea of his movements before Janice was attacked. I think it’s time we see if we can track him down ourselves,” I proclaimed.

“Do you think we’re strong enough to confront him?”

I held my hand out toward the grass fluttering in the afternoon breeze. With a small sigh of relief, I felt my magic snap to attention as I twisted my fingers in a braiding motion and tugged. The grass shot up like a weed, winding around itself to fulfill my intent to form a slender rope of grass. I directed it toward the railing, and it wound its way through, tightening until it formed a solid knot.

Beside me, Piper turned her hand over, palm up and a little spark of flame jumped off her skin, dancing along each fingertip before she snuffed it out. A sense of belonging hit me hard in the chest seeing our magic side-by-side. A voice in the back of my head that sounded distinctly like Nan told me that together, we could be a formidable force.

"Yeah, I'd say we're strong enough," I answered and took her hand to pull her to her feet.

Time to track down Janice's murderer.

12

––––––

I produced the fob watch from my pocket, turning the dark metal over in my fingers. I had no idea how it was meant to work and had neglected to ask Tyson for details. I'd been clearly overconfident in my acceptance of his deal.

"Any idea how it's supposed to work?" Piper asked.

"Not a bloody clue."

She took it from me and turned it over, laying it flat against her palm. She fiddled with something near where the chain connected to the object. I heard a soft 'click' as the face of the watch opened to reveal not a timepiece but a compass. A slender gold needle pointed unwavering toward north.

"I'll be honest, I've never been overly good with directions," I admitted.

"What if we just ask it to show us where to find Levi?"

I leaned over her hand and said as clearly as possible, "Please take us to where we can find Levi Sanders."

Nothing happened though. The needle remained firmly pointed to north and somehow, I doubted he was standing right in front of us. Then again, there was every chance he had mastered invisibility, too.

"Hang on, I've got an idea." I didn't bother explaining more to Piper before racing back inside. "Beau?" I whispered.

A small shimmer rippled along the bottom of the railing to reveal my chameleon companion lounging there. Somehow people never seemed to accidentally grab hold of him when he used the railing as his perch. Maybe he somehow telepathically compelled them to ignore him. He opened one eye lazily as I approached. I bent down and stroked the top of his head.

"Mate, I know I've asked a lot of you already, but I just need one more favor. I need you to come outside and tell me if you can sense anyone around."

Beau scurried up my outstretched forearm to perch on my shoulder, signaling his assent to what I was asking. I returned to the front steps and Piper eyed Beau with skepticism.

"You really think your pet can help?'

"He's not a pet. He's my ..." Beau and I had never really put a label on what we were. "More of a familiar, I suppose."

"And how is he going to help exactly? I thought you said he can turn invisible. Actually, given what we're about to do, that might not be a bad idea."

"That's one of Beau's many talents. He's also telepathic and can sense when other people are near," I explained and positioned my arm near the compass. "Mate, do you sense anyone out here with us?"

'All clear.'

"He says we're alone. Which means we're not using this thing correctly," I interpreted.

"So, we don't ask it to find the person we're looking for," Piper said, turning the object over in her hand again.

Beau darted like a lightning shot off my arm, catching his claws in the tender skin of my hand as he did so. I barely had time to hiss in pain before a drop of blood landed on the compass. He leapt to Piper's hand, and caught her with his claws, too. A second drop of blood joined mine, turning the crystalline face of the compass pink and hazy for a moment. When Beau transitioned back to my arm, he used his weight to move my hand so that it brushed Piper's.

"Uh, I'm guessing we both need to be doing something here," Piper noted.

I agreed. But what exactly?

"Get out your phone. Find a clear photo of him," I said, moving my hand so that it supported hers.

She fished her phone from her pocket and pulled up one of her social media accounts, navigating until she found Levi's profile. She held a photo that he'd taken at one of the other shows by the location tag listed on the post. I did my best to commit his image to memory and took a deep breath.

Okay, compass, let's see if we can retrace his steps.

"Uh, Darcy, it's doing something."

I looked at the compass to see the needle spinning wildly, finally landing on east. I pictured the town's layout in my head. Heading in that direction would take us past Tyson's shop and beyond the town boundary. Not something we could do easily on foot. I'd learned that the hard way once before.

"We're going to need to drive," I announced.

The front door opened behind us, and I heard the telltale jangle of keys in someone's hand. I pivoted to see Tania holding out the keys to her VW Bug. "Just don't get into any accidents," she noted with a small wink as she handed them over.

"Maybe I should drive?" Piper offered with a skeptical look, but I shook my head.

"It's an inside joke. The very first time I visited town, I stayed at Tania's. We were on our way to see a fireworks display on the pier and we got hit by a getaway driver."

"You weren't kidding when you said you keep getting mixed up in things in this town," Piper said with a small smirk as we climbed into the VW Bug.

"I swear I don't try to find trouble. It just seems to have a knack for finding me."

'Heart of a detective.'

I suppose I do. I secured my seatbelt and revved the engine.

Piper placed the compass in the center console. I could see through the pink smear that the needle still pointed east. Getting out of the driveway was an exercise in creativity as I maneuvered around the troupe's many cars and vans. Before long though, we were on the road, following the compass's direction.

It felt strange not to be following my own magic,

but I was buoyed by Piper's company. Hopefully, the family that sleuthed together would turn out to be the family that stayed together.

"I wasn't in charge of booking accommodations, but I didn't get the sense there were many places to stay around here," Piper noted as the compass led us past Tyson's shop and onto the main road leading to the highway and away from Brookhaven.

"Tania's is really the only place in town for folks to stay within town limits. But there are a couple of motels within about five to ten minutes drive. If I had to guess, I'd say Levi is holed up in one of those."

Given the lengths it appeared he had gone to in order to slip backstage, I had no doubt he'd have figured out where the troupe would be staying during their performances here. Showing up at the same place as a guest would have been a surefire way to get himself arrested. So, he'd need to be far enough away they might not see him out and about, but close enough to get to the theater when he wanted.

"What do we do if he's there?" Piper asked as the compass needle shifted again and I made a hard right turn onto a small service road with a sign for a cheap motel.

"We call the police and let them handle it," I answered.

Part of me feared that Levi would be there since the compass was supposed to lead us to where he was. At least it hadn't dragged us all over town to every place he'd visited since his arrival. The compass needle continued pointing straight as the road wound through trees to reveal a small three-story building with a handful of parking spaces.

"I'm guessing this place doesn't do a lot of business," Piper said as we left the car behind and approached the front door of the hotel. I stowed the compass in my pocket, checking it before crossing the threshold. I realized too late we should have discussed a plan or some sort of ruse to tell anyone we came across about why we were there.

A heavyset man with a bald spot on the top of his head sat behind the counter flipping through a magazine. He didn't acknowledge our presence even as the door swung shut behind me with a loud 'thud.' I took a moment to survey the space. There was a sign on the wall that boasted internet for $20 per night and single rooms for $50. I waved Piper over to where I stood by the sign.

"Should we ask for a room?"

"I get the feeling this isn't the type of place that

likes to take credit cards and I don't have any money on me." She glanced over her shoulder. "Wait, I've got a better idea."

She approached the desk and made a show of ringing the bell perched on the edge. It made a satisfying clang and the man looked up from his reading material. "Rates are on the wall."

"We were actually hoping you might be able to help us with something else," Piper replied, batting her lashes at him.

"What sort of help?"

"My brother took off on some crazy cross-country trip. He's trying to impress a girl and she was on vacation around here. We tried to talk him out of it, but he just left … and we've only been able to track him to this area, because of his social media post," Piper said in one big breath.

It pulled heavily from the truth which I suspected made it easier for her to be convincing.

"And we're afraid he's going to do something when she rejects him," Piper continued. "We've been stopping at every hotel and motel on the highway to see if he's there." She showed him the image of Levi on her phone. "Have you seen him?"

The man's gaze narrowed and his brows furrowed. If I were in his position, I'd be weighing the risk of providing customer information to two strangers. My heart thumped painfully against my ribs as we waited for him to make a decision.

"Might have seen him. Came in yesterday. Wasn't interested in a room. Just the internet."

"Thank you," Piper gushed. "We really appreciate your help."

She was out the door to the parking lot before I could ask any other questions. I hurried to catch up with my cousin as we headed back to the VW Bug. "Why would he only need internet?"

Piper pointed to the only other vehicle in the lot. "Looks like he's got a camper and is driving it across country."

I slid the compass from my pocket and checked the needle. It pointed northwest, right at the camper. Looks like we'd found Janice's stalker. I made sure my phone was easily within reach before we approached. The curtains on the camper were drawn as I walked the perimeter. There was only one door and when I tried the latch, it opened with a soft 'click.' Two steps led into the camper proper and past the driver seat.

The fact that no one had come to see who'd opened the door signaled he wasn't there now. Swallowing my nerves, I marched up the two steps and found the interior a mess of paper and playbills.

"You better come in here," I called out to Piper.

The camper groaned under her added weight as she stepped inside. I heard the door shut behind her. "Oh, okay this is a whole different level of crazy." She hooked a thumb over her shoulder toward the front of the vehicle. "It feels like the engine is still warm. So, he must have come back here recently."

"Where is he now then?"

"No idea. Let's be quick."

I picked up printed photos of Janice on stage in different costumes. Sometimes she was dressed in street clothes with her hair tossed up in a messy knot. There was nothing to suggest when the photos were taken. And given the fact the troupe used the same scenery backdrops; I doubted Piper would recognize specific venues.

"See anything that might suggest he magically poisoned the props?" I asked as I navigated around stacks of printed pages toward the lone bunk in the back. Levi certainly wasn't one for neatness.

"No. And I'm not getting any of those same vibes as I did before."

"Neither am I."

I made it to the very back of the camper to find a

toilet and sink. There was a bag stuffed between the toilet and the wall. I bent down the free it, careful to wrap my hand in the hem of my shirt first.

"Piper, I think you'll want to see this."

I backed out of the cramped space and turned to show my cousin the bag Levi had been sporting in the most recent social media photo. She undid the clasp holding it closed to reveal the delivery uniform, gloves, a wig, and glasses.

"He was definitely trying to avoid detection."

As Piper moved to peer out the window facing the row of first-floor motel rooms, I took a closer look at some of the papers stacked on the tiny table attached to the wall. They appeared to be printouts of messages, but not from any site I recognized. Some could have been texts.

"We need to go." Piper's voice jumped an octave as she spoke.

Using my phone camera, I took a flurry of photos of the top few messages on the table before pulling Piper to the front of the camper. As the curtain fluttered back into place, I spotted Levi walking out of one of the motel rooms with a phone pressed to his ear.

"Beau, mate, now would be a grand time for a bit of camouflage."

I clasped my hand firmly on Piper's wrist and felt the warmth of Beau's magic envelope us both. Piper's reflection in the rearview mirror blinked out of sight just as the door opened and Levi stood, half in the camper. I held my breath, squeezing Piper's wrist like a vice.

"You're lying. I would know if Janice was gone. I would *feel* it," he told whoever was on the other end of the line. "No, I'll see for myself."

There was another pause as whoever was on the other end of the phone spoke. "You haven't steered me wrong, yet. But I think you'd screw me if it meant you didn't get what you wanted."

I stumbled into the passenger seat closest to the door and hauled Piper into my lap. Levi ended the call and bounded inside the camper, heading straight for the back. I shoved Piper forward out of my lap and to her credit, she didn't make a sound as I felt her stumble on the steps. Still holding fast, we scurried toward Tania's car as Levi stuck his head out the open doorway. He looked past where we stood and vanished back inside.

We waited until the camper had pulled out of the parking lot before we dared let Beau's magic fade and climb into the VW Bug. My heart hammered in my chest, making it difficult to breathe, even as I processed the fact we had narrowly avoided getting caught.

"You heard that right?" Piper said as I put the car in drive, and started the trek back to Tania's B&B.

"Yeah, he's not working alone."

There was someone else within the production providing Levi access to the theaters and to Janice specifically. That complicated matters and meant we had likely been sharing meals with an accomplice to murder. Drawing them both out at the vigil would be our best move.

nxiety that had nothing to do with the magic I'd encountered the day before tightened my stomach as Piper and I walked back inside. The sun had already gone past the horizon. I could smell the scent of garlic bread baking in the oven while two large pots of pasta boiled on the stove. Tania was nothing if not versatile in her culinary tastes. I ushered Piper upstairs to my bedroom.

"What do we do now?" she asked.

"Can you think of anyone who would want to help Levi? Anyone who thought it was sort of sweet or something?"

"No, everyone hates him. Like, people don't get along in most productions, but everyone agreed that Levi was a creep." She threw herself down across my bed. "Do you think he's going to the hospital to try and see her body?"

I shuddered at the thought. "Who knows? Maybe we'll get lucky, and the police will snatch him up for questioning while he's there and save us all the trouble."

"Just the two officers in this town? Seems a little unlikely," Piper answered.

I sat beside her and made a grabbing motion toward her phone. "We still need to tag him for the vigil. We can't assume whoever he's working with is going to let him know. Besides, it sounds like there might be some kind of breakdown in their relationship given what Levi just said."

Piper levered herself into a sitting position and opened her social media app. She scrolled through some photos in her camera feed until she found one that showed both her and Janice. It looked to be during a costume fitting. They were posed back to back with matching grins.

"For all the talk of her being high maintenance, it looked like the pair of you got on sometimes," I pointed out.

"She wasn't all bad. She took her craft seriously, it's just I think she took it a little too seriously at times," Piper replied. "But she didn't deserve this."

"No, she didn't."

I watched as Piper composed her post. She would type a few words, delete them, and start over. Finally, she settled on:

NOT HOW I THOUGHT THIS TOUR WOULD GO. WE ARE ALL STUNNED BY @THEJANICE27'S DEATH. SUCH A SHOCK TO LOSE SOMEONE SO YOUNG. JOIN US FOR A VIGIL AT BROOKHAVEN'S THESPIAN HOUSE TOMORROW NIGHT AT FIVE O'CLOCK. COME LET HER LIGHT SHINE ON ALL OF US ONE FINAL TIME. #CASTMATE #RIP #NEVERFORGOTTEN.

She looked at me before she posted. "Do you think that's good enough?'

"It gives the information he would need and if he's not caught by Chief Hayes or the morgue staff today, he'll definitely show up."

She posted it and we waited, watching for any notifications. Likes and comments came faster than I would have anticipated. Most people expressed their shock and asked for more details. Piper didn't give them. You didn't need to be a police officer to know disseminating information during an active investigation was a bad idea. Especially when we were doing what we could to divert the police's attention away from Piper.

There wasn't much else to do now besides wait

and hope that Levi would take the bait. Still there was the matter of determining who might be his inside accomplice. But short of starting to question everyone in the B&B, I wasn't sure where else to start. And I kept trying to remind myself that this wasn't my job. I tended marijuana plants, didn't solve murders.

I settled back against the pillows, staring up at the ceiling as Piper still lay sprawled across the bed in the other direction. It was nice to just sit in the quiet with someone who shared more than just magic with me. I felt the mattress shift and looked to see her propping her chin in her hand.

"What?" I asked, feeling suddenly self-conscious.

"Nothing. You've just got this sort of faraway look," she commented.

"Just thinking about how nice it is to have family close by. Someone I can actually talk to about all this magic stuff without being told I'm losing it."

"Yeah, it is."

"You've got your mum though. I'm sure she talks to you about it."

"Not really. I mean, she tries really hard to blend in. It's why we didn't really talk about it with anyone in the cast. She wanted us to seem normal."

"Maybe it's just the older generation?" I suggested and sat back up.

"Maybe. I wish I could be more open with mine. Sometimes I feel like I've got all this power and energy inside me that just needs to come out ... and I can't let it," she admitted.

"That's how I felt when my powers first manifested. I couldn't walk down the street without the plants in people's window boxes calling out to me. But the more I used it, the better I got at controlling it."

Piper looked down at her hands. "Showing you my magic earlier was the most I've done in months."

"I've got an idea. Come with me."

I levered myself off the bed and held out a hand to pull her up. She gave me a tentative look before accepting it. I didn't give her a chance to ask any more questions as I guided her out the front door and toward the boardwalk. It was mostly deserted this time of year, what with the water making the area even colder. A couple of people strolled along closer to town. Still, I kept going until I reached the far end of the pier.

"Why are we out here?" Piper looked around.

"You need to let your power out. Directing it into the water will make sure nothing accidentally catches fire. And no one's out here, so if you're worried about anyone seeing, they won't."

"I don't know ..."

"You shouldn't have to feel like you can't exist in your own skin."

"Uh ... What if it's too much power?"

I gestured to the expanse of water in front of us. "It's a lot of water. I think it can take it."

Piper inhaled and held out one hand, palm up. Flames rippled across her skin as if she'd flicked on a series of lighters. They were small, undulating feebly in the wind. The light reflected in my cousin's eyes, and I could see there was a hunger there ready to let loose.

"Don't be afraid," I encouraged.

"I spent a lot of time being labeled things I wasn't because of my magic," she said in a hushed voice.

"You are a witch. You've got to own your power. If I've learned anything in the last year, it's that."

I held my own hand out and felt power course through me, seeking anything flora that it could attach itself to. I didn't have to search very hard. There were aquatic plants hidden beneath the surface of the water. With a little encouragement, they shot up, twisting and winding themselves together into a slender braid. Using a bit more coaxing it grew offshoots, expanding into various undulating knots of seaweed and kelp.

"If you need something to aim at."

Piper's face turned into a mask of determination as the fire in her hand coalesced into a white-hot ball of fire. She drew her hand back and lobbed it at one of the knots. It collided with a hiss and the plant matter withered and dropped back into the water.

"That was for framing me," Piper shouted into the empty air.

In quick succession, two more fire balls were sailing through the air, making contact with their targets. I felt a twinge of sadness at the loss of life, but I knew it was for a purpose. Piper wouldn't be able to control or even enjoy her magic if she didn't let out all of the frustration pent up inside of her.

"That's for ruining this part of my life." Her voice shifted from yelling into a sob and her knees gave out.

I managed to catch her before she hit the wooden planks, easing her down gently. I let her sit there, clinging to me as she cried. Her skin felt warm to the touch, almost feverish. When she finally pulled away from me, her cheeks were flushed. When she brushed the tears away, they sizzled and turned to steam on the backs of her knuckles. That same tension I'd noticed in her shoulders when she came back from the police station was still there and it stretched upward, making the muscles on the sides of her neck taut with frustration.

"I think you might have a little more to get out," I said.

Wordlessly, Piper got back to her feet, held out both hands in front of her and fire shot from every pore, funneling into a giant ball of energy. She opened her mouth and a guttural roar ripped from her throat. The flames finally stopped flowing and the magic she'd poured out dropped into the ocean to be swallowed up by the waves and rendered harmless.

"Thank you," she finally said once she'd caught her breath.

"That's what family's for." I answered.

"Let's hope I don't need to do that again anytime soon."

"I think you should talk to Tania about what you've been feeling."

She fixed me with a quizzical look. "The B&B owner?"

"She's an empath. And she's been helping me learn to harness and hone my magic since I moved here."

"You think she could help?"

"At the very least, she'd literally know what you're going through and feeling. She might have some suggestions on how to work through it."

"Why not. I'll give it a try."

The walk back to Tania's was quick and we found her sitting in the backyard sipping a cup of tea. I offered a small wave to get her attention. "Mind if we join you?'

"Of course not. Please, sit."

I plunked myself down on the grass, giving Piper the other chair. I wound my fingers through the blades of grass. They were still nascent, almost seedlings and not fully formed yet. Absently, I poured a little power into them, urging them to grow.

"I don't know what you two have been doing, but I can sense relief wafting off you," Tania noted, setting her teacup down.

"Oh, Darcy realized I was holding a lot of stuff in, and I needed to just let it out," Piper answered.

"Like magic?"

Piper's gaze darted around us, as if fearing we might be overheard by the wrong people. "Um, yes."

"I am glad you were able to get it out. Letting it build, and continually trying to contain it, just like anything else, can be harmful to you. Not only because magic can sometimes become unpredictable, especially elemental magic, but it can affect you in other ways. Mentally and physically."

"So, I'm learning. Getting questioned by the police certainly didn't help things," Piper said.

"I trust Darcy shared my particular skills with you?"

"She said you're an empath."

"Okay, so when I say I know what you are feeling, I am not speaking metaphorically. I literally feel what you do. I sense there is still some unresolved tension under the surface."

"It's not about my magic. I get that I need to nurture it and find ways to learn to control it safely. It's just what happened to Janice. I know I'll be expected to be the female lead once we start back up. But it feels wrong. Like I don't want the role anymore."

"That sounds like a discussion you should be having with your director," Tania noted.

"But I also don't want to let anyone down," Piper sighed.

"You can only be responsible for yourself," Tania said, reaching over to pat Piper's hand. "Now, where did the two of you race off to earlier with my car?"

"We may have found Janice's stalker," I admitted.

"*Dios Mio.*"

"He didn't see us. Thankfully."

"But he's definitely obsessed with her. We think he might have been on his way to the hospital to see her," Piper added.

"And we overheard him talking to someone. It sounds like he might have an accomplice within the troupe," I shared, the grass shoots arching over my knuckles, forming tiny bridges. I looked at Tania, her dark eyes locked on mine. "Have you sensed anything duplicitous going on with anyone?"

"Honestly, I've been feeling mostly grief the last two days," Tania answered. "If there is someone who is hiding things, they are doing a very good job of it."

"We think at least Levi used magic to kill Janice," I said. "So, maybe he found a way to block you from detecting his accomplice?"

"That is possible. After all, it wouldn't be the first time someone has been able to use magic to obscure my abilities."

Tania looked at me and my mind flashed to the drama from six months ago. Andrew Webster's daughter had managed to conceal her magic and motives from Tania. If I hadn't gone snooping, it was possible she would have gotten away with killing her father, and the man's host of ex-wives would have taken the fall.

"Well, we've put out a lure for Janice's stalker, assuming that Chief Hayes doesn't catch up with him at the morgue," I said, redirecting the discussion. "We're hoping he'll show up at the vigil tomorrow night."

"That is risky without letting Rick or Vinnie know."

My gut told me that Chief Hayes didn't want our help. But he might be more willing to take the hint from someone a little closer to home. Ginny and I weren't exactly friends these days, but she had asked me to nudge the police chief in the right direction before. Maybe I could get her to return the favor?

Tania looked back through the window into the kitchen. I could see by the slight slump of her shoulders she was thinking about the fact she needed to go cook for the grieving throng of people inside.

"Why don't you let me handle dinner tonight," I said.

"You aren't exactly the best in the kitchen," she retorted.

"No, but I'm sure Ginny wouldn't mind fixing up some plates for folks. Besides, I've been meaning to test out their takeaway menu."

She didn't protest or ask if I had any ulterior motives. That was good. The grass shoots receded to their normal-for-March length, allowing me to stand up. Piper looked exhausted as she sat there in the afternoon air. I'd let her rest.

"I'll just get a little of everything?"

"That should do just fine. But here, let me at least give you some money," Tania said, gesturing in the direction of the kitchen. "There's some emergency money under the cutlery."

I found the money and peeled off a block of twenty dollar bills, shoving them into my pocket. "I'll be back."

I reached the front hall and felt a presence behind me. I turned to find Sam hovering there. "Keep an eye on them for me, yeah? There's someone staying here we can't trust."

"I'd say I'd guard them with my life, but..." Sam gestured to his incorporeal form. "But I'll haunt the living crap out of anyone who comes at them."

Time to pay the town's very own human lie detector a visit.

14

———

Ginny's was bustling when I walked in shortly before six o'clock. The owner sat in her usual place of honor, with a stool conveniently vacant beside her. She pivoted in her seat when I entered and gestured for me to join her.

"I'm not staying long," I told her as she shoved a takeout menu at me. "Did Tania call you?"

"She thought it was polite to let me know to expect a big takeout order," Ginny answered. "Also, she hinted that there was something you might want to talk to me about."

"I do, actually. First, I wanted to say thanks for letting Piper get a good meal in her earlier before your brother took her away for questioning."

"I didn't get assault vibes from her. But I know how stressful being in a room with Rick can be."

"We're fairly certain we know who attacked Janice, and even sort of the how. We've set a bit of a lure for culprit, but we figured it would be good if the police knew what was happening."

"Hmm ... and you don't think my brother would take it well coming from you."

"Can you blame me? I'm not exactly his favorite person in town. And I swear I don't go looking to get mixed up in things. It just kind of happens."

"Some people are just murder magnets," Ginny answered with a smirk.

I didn't care for the label, but I also couldn't deny the truth of it. People just kept dying around me. For once I'd like to happen upon something good like a newborn baby, or maybe a litter of adorable puppies in need of a good home.

"Do you think you could float it to him, that Janice's stalker is likely to show up to the vigil tomorrow?"

"I can let him know."

"You wouldn't happen to know if he's actually followed up on the information Piper provided them about this bloke?"

Ginny let out a snort. "Please, Rick purposely

avoids me when he's working on a case. He knows I'd pull too much out of him I shouldn't know."

"If I were in his shoes, I'd be putting your particular skills to use as often as possible," I remarked.

"Don't think I haven't tried. And yes, I feed him information from time to time if someone spills a naughty secret I think he should know about, but he prefers to do his work the mundane way."

I pulled my phone from my pocket and navigated to Levi's social media profile. "You haven't seen him come through, have you?"

I half-expected Ginny to give the image only a cursory glance, but she studied his face, enlarging the image to stare into his eyes. "I don't think so. But that's your guy?"

"Yeah. He'd been harassing the victim for months, following her on tour to every place they went. Sending her messages online. I talked to some of the backstage crew, and they confirmed seeing someone rummaging around the theater on the night of the attack. Then Piper and I found some costume items in his camper for a disguise."

"You went looking for him?"

"We needed to know how viable a suspect he was if we wanted Rick to lay off Piper." I toyed with the edge of the takeout menu. "And we did. From what

I've heard about him, he's not only obsessed with Janice, but with the Romeo and Juliet story. For all we know he's going to try and hurt himself when he finds out Janice is dead."

"That's macabre," she whispered.

"I know I don't have any right to ask you for a favor, but would you consider coming to the vigil tomorrow? Just to see if we can get him to actually confess?"

"I'm not a miracle worker. Like most witches with powers linked to emotions, we're not infallible. But I want this psycho caught and out of my town as badly as you do. So yes, I'll come."

"Thank you."

"Now, how about you order what you came for. You've got a house full of hungry thespians to feed."

"I'll take two of everything," I said, sliding the menu back to her and took out the money from Tania's stash.

Ginny eyed the wad of bills and said, "The bill's more than what you brought. But since it's for Tania and these aren't normal circumstances, I'll give you a discount." She plucked the money from my hand and disappeared into the kitchen to place the order.

Twenty minutes later, Ginny reappeared carrying a large box packed with four large paper bags. She slid it across the counter toward me. "Enjoy. And I'll see you tomorrow. Please try to stay out of trouble in the meantime."

"I'll do my best."

I felt better returning to the B&B having talked to Ginny. At least we had a chance of getting Levi to confess with her coming to the vigil. Besides, there was still a possibility the police had already arrested him for trying to do who-knows-what to Janice's body. And if we're lucky, maybe Ginny's presence would draw out Levi's accomplice and we could return to our murder-free existence.

DINNER WAS A QUIET AFFAIR, guests taking their food and drifting off into small groups to eat in silence. It appeared everyone was still processing the truth that Janice was dead. At least they'd mostly stopped shooting daggers at Piper. She looked almost rested when she slipped in behind me at the counter as I plunked chicken wings down onto my plate.

"So, I had an idea," she said in my ear.

"What kind?"

"Well, Lucy was probably Janice's biggest fan

from the troupe. I wouldn't put it past her to collaborate with another fan."

"Yeah, but she looked genuinely upset about Janice getting attacked and killed," I reminded her.

"But we know they're having some sort of split. What if it went too far for her? Or she might know who secretly had it out for Janice. Either way, we should talk to her."

"She kind of hates you, though," I added.

"That's why I'm not going to talk to her alone," she answered and looped her arm through mine, tugging me away from the counter.

We wound our way through the clusters of troupe members to find Lucy standing by one of the windows in the living room overlooking the front yard. She held a cup in one hand, the other wrapped tight around her torso. The way her body swayed, I suspected she had been crying. When she turned at our approach, the smeared mascara confirmed my hunch.

"What do you want?" She glared at Piper.

"I know you don't like me, Lucy. I honestly don't get why. But I swear to you I didn't do anything to Janice. And I am really sorry she's dead."

Lucy wiped her eyes with the back of her hand,

her knuckles coming away with smudges. "I guess I have been kind of mean to you."

"She was your friend; and you're grieving. It's still fresh," I said, hoping to ease the tension.

"She was my best friend." She took a shaky breath. "Everyone thought I was mad about being relegated to the background. I wasn't. I just didn't like having to share my best friend with everyone. But I knew she was supposed to be the star."

"I'm guessing you two spent a lot of time together," I probed. "Like running lines and such?"

"Sometimes. But honestly, Janice just wanted to do non-theater stuff when we hung out. She called it her slice of normal. We'd watch old horror movies together. No one really knew that she loved those."

"Well, now someone else knows that about her. Thank you for sharing that," Piper said. "Do you think I could ask you something that's kind of personal?"

"I guess."

"I know we all knew about Levi, but you probably knew more about him than most. Did he ever show up anywhere else?" Piper pressed, directing the conversation more gently than I'd have expected.

"Somehow that creep got her home address, and he showed up there once. But he took off before we could call the police. It was maybe six months ago. She'd been staying with me since then. Just to be safe."

"Did you know he showed up here?" I noted. "He posted it on social media."

"Honestly, I don't know how he keeps getting in," she said, her hand tightening around her cup.

"Do you think someone in the cast or crew might have let him in?" Piper's words were blunt.

"No way." Her gaze went unfocused for a moment. "Well ... I mean, not that he'd have done anything like that, but I know Benji tried to deal with him a few times when Celia was busy. But I'm sure he was just warning him off."

"Thanks," I said, tugging Piper away. "Benji's your mate who runs the lights, right?"

"He's harmless. He's a bit awkward, but he didn't have anything against Janice."

"But I heard him call her for the end of intermission right before she went back on stage. Maybe he knows something?"

Piper looked around the room. "I don't see him. But that's not unusual. He isn't really a crowd person. It's why he's happy in the lighting booth."

"Do you think he'd be upstairs then?"

"Probably."

I ushered her to the front entrance and checked the logbook to find his room number: 10. We made our way up to the third floor and spotted the door to Room 10 ajar. I could hear fabric moving within and took a step in front of Piper as we approached.

"Benji?" Piper called from behind me.

The door opened and Benji stuck his head out. "What do you—oh, hey Piper. Sorry, didn't realize it was you."

"We were just wondering if you wanted something to eat," I lied.

"No, I'm fine. Thanks."

"Okay." Piper made a show of starting to turn back toward the stairs. "Actually, can we ask you something?"

"I guess."

"From what people are saying, I guess they've heard some rumblings from the police, they're looking at Levi Sanders. You had a of couple run-ins with him before, right?"

"Doesn't sound familiar."

"Janice's stalker?" I prompted.

"Oh, right, him. I guess I might have seen him once or twice."

"You didn't interact with him at all?" I pushed, taking a step closer to the door.

"If you haven't noticed, I don't really like being around people. So, I tend to avoid them wherever possible. If I did see him or talked to him, it wouldn't have been for long. But if it was the guy who'd kept showing up, I probably told him to get lost."

"That's what I thought," Piper said. "Thanks. Have a good night, Benji."

"Night, Piper."

I ushered my cousin back down to her room. There was something a little off about our interaction with Benji, but I couldn't put my finger on it. Piper had said he was socially awkward. But his answers didn't fit with what Lucy had just told us. The fact neither Chief Hayes nor Vinnie had come by with any updates on the case worried me, too. Had Levi managed to slip past hospital security?

"You look worried," Piper said, pulling me from my mental spiral.

"Sorry, just something about all this feels off."

"Maybe we were wrong, and it wasn't someone in the cast or crew, and he just got really lucky?" Piper said, picking up a phone on the bed beside her.

She looked down at it, and after a moment of repeatedly entering her password to no avail let out a sigh. "Mom."

"What about your mum?"

"She's always leaving her phone around and she got the same case as mine. So, I sometimes forget it's not mine when I pick it up."

"We haven't asked your mum if she's seen anything out of the ordinary."

"She's been kind of MIA all afternoon," Piper noted.

Her focus returned to the phone, and she entered a different code. The screen unlocked to reveal a photo of Audrey and Piper at a theater with a thick billowing red curtain behind them. I noticed a missed text just as Piper tapped on the message icon to reveal a conversation with a number without a name.

> I think I'm finally ready to make the
> big move.

Piper scrolled back up through the conversation and her eyes widened as she did so. "Who is she talking to? These go back for months. It's like she's coaching someone on how to be romantic."

"You don't think she was the one feeding information to Levi, do you?"

"No way. Not a chance." Her face fell. "She did really want me to get the lead role though."

"So, let's go ask her. I'm sure she can sort this all out if you just talk to her."

She held out her hand to me. "Let me borrow the compass. I'll find her real quick."

"Or we wait and cool off first," I said, gesturing to her left hand as the plastic phone case started to smolder and warp.

She threw the phone onto the floor, staring at her hand as if expecting there to be a burn where her skin had touched the plastic. Her hand was unblemished. "Okay. You're probably right. Confronting her now only leads to me saying things I can't take back."

"We're going to sort this out, I promise," I said, pulling her into a one-armed hug.

We parted ways not long after and I returned to my own room, settling in for the night. I'd sent Maggie a brief text to fill her in on what we'd learned since I'd seen her last. She warned me to be careful and I assured her I would try. Beau turned one judgmental eye toward me as he curled up on one of the pillows.

"I haven't gotten injured or arrested this time around. I think we're doing pretty well," I told him as I climbed beneath the covers.

Around me, I could just make out the muffled

voices of our various guests begin to dwindle as they, too, turned in for the night. I wasn't an empath by any stretch, but I could still feel Piper's anxiety about the messages on her mum's phone as I drifted off to sleep. I could only imagine Tania's stress level if she was anywhere near my cousin.

I'd barely slipped into a fitful sleep when something woke me. At first, disorientation gripped me, and I thrashed around in the dark until my momentum sent me tumbling out of bed. The collision with the floor was enough to jolt me awake and I quickly found the light switch by the door. The familiarity of my bedroom eased the galloping speed of my pulse for a brief moment until the sound that had woken me happened again—breaking glass.

Someone was breaking in the B&B.

15

Panic froze me in place as my mind spun out like a car hitting black ice. If I'd heard the glass breaking, that meant they had to be trying to get in somewhere nearby. The B&B wasn't that accessible, and the bedrooms were mostly positioned facing the backyard. If someone was trying to get in through a window, it likely had to be through the front windows or maybe the front door.

If I'd woken to the sound, who else was awake now? Taking a deep breath, I managed to get my arms to obey my mind's directive to move. I grabbed my phone and tugged it from the charging cable. The screen lit up, showing it was 2:18 in the morning. Whoever was trying to gain entry was brazen.

Break-ins were not a common occurrence in Brookhaven. Most folks left their doors unlocked and trusted their neighbors. It wasn't a phenomenon I could really get behind, but I wasn't the one in charge at the B&B. Which also begged the question of why someone would feel the need to smash glass to get in?

"Come on, Darcy. Do something," I urged myself.

It took more determination than I thought reasonable to get my feet to move. Once they did, my first instinct was to thunder down the hall to Tania's room and wake her. She needed to know what was happening. But that would betray my presence and could scare off our intruder. My gut told me it had to be Levi. No one else would have a reason to sneak in. Alerting Tania was still the best first move, but I needed to proceed with caution and stealth. I pressed myself to the wall opposite my room and inched down the hall to the master bedroom. The door was shut tight.

"Tania?" I called out in as loud a voice as I dared.

No reply.

"Sam?" I tried a little louder.

Our resident ghost wasn't aways present at night. He liked to go out and about during the early hours and often spent his mornings watching the sunrise. I had to hope that given we were in the midst of a murder investigation; he'd stuck close to home.

"Why are you awake?" His voice came from behind me.

"Oh, thank God you're still here," I said, pivoting to face his translucent form. "I heard breaking glass. I think someone's trying to get into the house." Just then something went 'thud' above me.

"You may be a witch, but this is when you should call the police and let them do their job," Sam chided. He floated upward through the ceiling and disappeared.

I hesitated as I started to dial 9-1-1. Would they believe me if I told them what I suspected? It didn't matter. They'd have to come. I just needed to keep whoever was lurking upstairs around until they arrived. So, I finished dialing and pressed the phone to my ear.

"Brookhaven Police, please state your emergency," Vinnie answered after the second ring. I could hear the yawn in his voice on the word emergency.

"Vinnie, it's Darcy Ingram. There's someone breaking in at Tania's B&B. Please, you need to come."

"Find somewhere safe and whatever you do, Darcy, don't confront them."

"Just hurry," I said and ended the call before he could protest that I had to stay on the line until help arrived.

We had a house full of vulnerable guests and a potential turncoat in our midst. This was my home, and I was going to defend it. Tania still needed to know what was happening. So, I steeled myself, opening the door and walked into her room. It wasn't a space I visited often, and, in the darkness, it felt like an obstacle course. I stubbed my toe hard on the foot of the bed and barely kept from yelling out a string of colorful words before I'd reached my landlady.

"Tania, you need to wake up," I said as loud as I dared.

She sat up, looking around and I could see the whites of her eyes through the dimness when she turned to look at me. Her hands clamped down on my mine so tight I thought she would cut off my circulation. "Someone is in the house."

"I know. The police are on the way," I said.

"The guests ..." Tania said, throwing herself out of bed.

"It sounds like whoever broke in is upstairs," I

explained as I moved to follow her back into the hall.

"Janice's room was upstairs," Tania said, putting the pieces of the puzzle together before me.

I didn't give her time to object to my attempt to be heroic as I moved toward the stairs. As I put my foot on the first riser, the wood groaned beneath my weight, and I heard the soft click of a door opening. I moved back from the step to find Piper looking bleary-eyed at me.

"What's going on?"

"Someone's in the house. Go back into your room."

"It could be Levi. No way I'm letting you face that creep alone. Remember, we're stronger together," Piper hissed.

If my presence had been enough to make the wood on the stairs groan, both of us ascending to the third floor would give us away far too easily. Luckily, Tania's insistence of filling the house with plants for me to practice with meant there were some vines creeping out of a hanging pot nearby. They would do.

I moved next to it and dipped my fingers into the soil to find the plant's roots. Almost instantly I was hit with a rush of energy and excitement. Somehow this plant knew I was about to ask it for help and was ready to offer whatever it could.

"I'm going to need you to grow, and fast," I whispered. In my mind's eye, I pictured the vines carpeting the stairs to muffle our footsteps. As I opened my eyes again, I felt the vines slither across my wrists and wind down to the floor.

They snaked across the staircase, carpeting the wood in thick leafy vines. I tested one step and to my relief there was no sound. I led the way up to the third floor, the vines rippling out ahead of us like a red carpet. My adrenaline spiked as I realized Sam was nowhere to be seen. I was certain he'd come up here to keep an eye on the things. Had he somehow confronted our intruder? Could Levi's magic harm ghosts, too?

A crash followed by a frustrated sob came from down the hall.

"That's the room Janice was in," Piper whispered from behind me. Her hand glowed a gentle yellow-orange hue as she used her magic to give us some better lighting.

There were fewer rooms on the third floor, and I thought I spotted Benji's door ajar, too. Had he gone to confront Levi, too? Well, only one way to find out. As we approached Janice's room, I listened for the telltale sound of emergency vehicle sirens. None came. Surely Vinnie and the chief would come in metaphorical guns blazing.

For the moment, though, it appeared we were still on our own. I flexed my fingers and felt some of the vines that had muffled our approach twine around my fingers, ready to be twisted into bonds to keep our intruder from escaping. Throwing caution to the wind, I burst into the room, flicking on the overhead light as I did so.

Brilliant move, Darcy, I thought as the sudden shift in light blinded me, too.

Black spots popped in my vision for a few seconds, resolving into Levi standing in the middle of the room, clutching what looked to be one of Janice's dresses. His eyes were red-rimmed and bloodshot from crying. Clearly, he'd learned the truth about his actions.

"Benji!" Piper exclaimed, rushing past me.

I turned to see the other man lying slumped against the bed, apparently unconscious with a gash on his forehead. Levi appeared oblivious, not even realizing the other man was occupying space in the room. I just had to buy us a little more time until the police arrived.

"You're Levi, right?" I said, holding out one hand,

while keeping the vines concealed in the other behind my back.

"She's gone," he sobbed. "She's really gone. My beautiful angel."

"I know. Now, I don't think you meant for this to happen," I said, taking a half step closer to him.

"All I ever wanted was to love her. To make her see just how wonderful she was."

"I'm sure she knew."

"She was blinded by their brainwashing," he answered, jabbing a finger in Piper's direction. "They were trying to stifle her."

"But she was the lead actress; one of the most important parts in the entire play."

"But they poisoned her mind. They made her think I wanted to hurt her. I'd never harm her."

"Like I said, I don't think you meant for her to get hurt. But sometimes, the things we think are showing love, are really hurting those we care about."

Come on, Vinnie. Where are you?

"You think I wanted to hurt her?" Another sob wracked his whole body, and it was then that I caught sight of something metallic sheathed in his hand. My stomach dropped as he pulled out a knife. It had a simple silver handle and couldn't have been more than four inches long. Still big enough to do serious damage. There was a thin stain of red along one side of the blade.

"I think you wanted to be with her, and you tried everything you could think of to achieve that desire," I replied.

"You even snuck in wearing disguises, so we wouldn't throw you out," Piper spat, standing to block Benji from view.

"Is it wrong I wanted to give her flowers? And see her on stage? She always shined so bright on stage."

"She didn't want your attention. Don't you get that?" Piper's fingers flared white-hot as her emotions bubbled to the surface.

We didn't need a firefight inside. There was already enough damage to the B&B from Levi's unauthorized entry. "How about everyone just calms down? Levi, why don't you put that knife down, yeah? We don't need anyone else to get hurt."

"What's the point?" he wailed, his grasp around the knife's hilt tightening. "I don't want to be in this world when she's gone."

Part of me should have expected this reaction. Given what I knew about the man—admittedly all of it was second hand—his obsession with Janice was closely followed by his love of Romeo and Juliet. His

Juliet was dead. It was now his turn to end his life to be with her in eternity. But taking his own life was the coward's way out.

I could swear I heard sounds coming from below us. They sounded like footsteps and muffled voices. I prayed that it was the police come to arrest Levi for his crimes. On the other side of the room Benji gave a soft moan as he started to regain consciousness.

"You're going to have to live in this world without her for a while longer," I finally said and thrust out the hand I'd been keeping concealed. The vines shot off my skin and cinched tight around Levi's wrists. They squeezed tight enough to force him to drop the knife.

Piper darted forward, scooping it up long enough to toss it across the room. The footsteps I'd picked up on grew louder and in moments, both Vinnie and Chief Hayes appeared in my peripheral vision brandishing their guns.

"Someone want to tell me what's going on here?" Chief Hayes asked.

"He broke in and it looks like he was going through Janice's things," I answered, still maintaining the vine's grip on the man's wrists.

"That was the suspect I was telling you about,

Chief," Vinnie said and turned to Levi. "You're a hard man to pin down."

Levi made an awkward lunging motion toward me and the officers—maybe in a bid to force their hand and get out of facing justice for what he'd done. Except a thin vein of flame unfurled across the hem of the dress he'd been clutching, tripping him up as he tried to move forward. With lightning fast reflexes, Chief Hayes had him flat on the floor, his hands pinned beneath his weight.

"You can let him go now," he told me.

I let my fingers go slack and slowly the vines unwound themselves from Levi's hands. I heard him give a sigh as the pressure released. It was only a momentary relief, because Chief Hayes yanked his hands behind his back, securing them in handcuffs.

"Levi Sanders, you are under arrest for murder and breaking and entering," he said, hauling Levi to his feet. He shoved the man ahead of him as he continued to read him his rights. At the doorway, the chief paused to look at Vinnie. "Make sure we get someone to take a look at the other guy."

"On it," Vinnie replied, pulling his phone out and dialing a number. "I am so sorry to wake you up right now, but we could use your help." I caught what I thought was Maggie's voice on the other end of the line sleepily agreeing to do what she could. "We're at Tania's," he explained and ended the call.

"You're going to want our statements," I preempted.

Vinnie gave me a tired look. "You're getting way too used to this, Darcy."

"Tell me about it." I gestured for him to step into the hall to give Benji more time to wake up and space for Maggie to tend his wound once she arrived. "I heard breaking glass and came up to investigate. We found Levi crying and ranting about Janice being gone," I explained. "Benji, he's one of the lighting guys on the crew, was unconscious with that gash on his head. It looked like Levi might try to hurt himself and that's when I did what I could to restrain him until you arrived."

"I'll just leave out the fact I told you to get somewhere safe, and not confront the intruder from my report."

"I appreciate that." After a moment, I added, "Thank you for taking Piper seriously when she shared the information about the stalker and for actually trying to follow up on Levi as a suspect."

"It's my job. If there's nothing else, I need to take Miss Hennessey's statement now."

"Uh, I don't feel so goo—" Piper said, her words

beginning to slur as her body swayed in the open space of the bedroom.

"Piper!"

I watched in horror as my cousin crumpled to the floor like an empty paper bag. Color drained from her cheeks in the harsh overhead light. I was on my knees at her side in seconds, frantically feeling for a pulse. It was there, thrumming along in her jugular vein, but it was starting to slow. Her skin flushed bright pink before she broke out into a sweaty sheen and her breathing became ragged.

This can't be happening again.

What had Levi done to her?

16

Time slowed as I tried to figure out what to do next. Vinnie was by my side, but my hearing had blocked out all other tones except for a high-pitched buzzing noise. I couldn't even begin to understand what he was saying. On the other side of me, Benji came to fully, sitting up. He pressed one hand to his head, blinked and then fell to his knees beside Piper.

I felt the vibration of footfalls on the flooring beneath me and turned to see Maggie standing there in the doorway, framed by the darkness of the hall-way. Her red hair was a tussled mess and there were the beginnings of dark circles under her eyes. She'd never looked more beautiful to me.

"Help her!" I called. At least that's what I'd intended to say. My ears still weren't working properly, and it came out as garbled nonsense.

Maggie moved me out of the way gently and started probing Piper's prone form. I felt more vibrations and looked to see Audrey appear, trying to fill the already cramped space. Tania managed to keep her out of the way, pulling her out of view. I watched Vinnie and Maggie converse, hands darting to emphasize their points as they talked.

Slowly the flow of conversation came back to me. When Maggie looked over and said, "We need to get her to the hospital now." I understood the words this time.

"Can you do anything?" The words came out in a whisper.

She held up Piper's wrist to show that she had a firm grip on my cousin. The fact that Maggie's brow was now covered in a thin layer of sweat suggested she was doing what she could. Together, Vinnie and Maggie moved Piper downstairs. Someone had called for an ambulance because one pulled into the driveway a few minutes later, whisking Piper and Benji off to the hospital. Maggie's assessment of how long he'd been unconscious suggested he needed to be checked for a concussion.

That left me without anyone else who'd witnessed Levi's descent into suicidal madness. There was no chance I could get back into the room to see what else he might have been going after. Or more importantly, what could have caused Piper to collapse.

Part of me realized even if I could get access to the bedroom, there was very little chance I'd find anything at 2:30 in the morning. I needed sleep. But with the police traipsing through and the ambulance sirens blaring, I doubted that would happen. I was more surprised their presence hadn't roused more of the guests. As the ambulance pulled away, I saw Bree and Andrea huddled at the top of the second-floor landing.

"What happened?" Bree asked, sounding far too awake for this time of night. Andrea stood just behind her.

"Someone broke in. Piper and Benji got banged up. They're heading to the hospital to get checked out," I answered, offering a version of the truth that wouldn't get me into trouble with Chief Hayes.

That seemed to satisfy their curiosity and they retreated back to their room. I made my way down to the kitchen to find Tania pouring hot water into two oversized mugs I recognized from Ginny's. There was a small image with the year etched on the fronts denoting them as holiday mugs from a few years ago. I pulled down a smaller mug and accepted the teapot.

Audrey sat at the kitchen table, bleary-eyed as Tania set the steeping mug in front of her. "This will help," she said, patting my aunt's hand.

I joined the older woman and stared into the dark contents of my own mug for a while before speaking. Piper would want me to clear whatever was happening with her mum. Audrey took a sip from the mug and looked me straight in the eye.

"What did you get her into?"

"Excuse me?"

"You two have been running around thick as thieves since you met."

"We were trying to get to know each other. There's nothing wrong with that. It's why I reached out in the first place. And I have no idea what happened to Piper just now."

"She was happy and safe before all of this ... before ..."

"I think everyone was a lot happier and safer before someone murdered the troupe's lead actress," I retorted. "All I tried to do was show that Piper was innocent. Because I don't think she's got a mean bone in her body, let alone capable of harming someone just for a role in a play."

Audrey's accusatory look faded. "No, she's one of the sweetest, kindest people I know."

"Look, we did find some things out that I don't think you're going to like," I said, taking a fortifying gulp of tea.

"Like what?"

"Like, Janice was attacked using magic. It looked like whatever spell it was, tricked her body into thinking it was exposed to peanuts. It made her think she was having a massive allergic reaction and her body just shut down."

Audrey took another few sips from her mug. "I still don't like talking about it so openly ... magic, I mean. It feels wrong to share something so personal."

"But it's wrapped up in what happened to Janice. And I think it might be what happened to Piper, too. Does she have any allergies?"

"No. Nothing like that. I mean, she was allergic to pollen or dust, but that's normal. Everyone's got those types of allergies."

I somehow doubted my cousin was suffering

from a hay fever overdose. But her body clearly had a reaction to whatever the mystery component might be. It wasn't normal for someone to fall unconscious with a fever within seconds. But it wasn't the first time I'd seen Piper's body react in that way to stress —from pent up anxiety.

"I know you don't like talking about magic, but we need to. Piper, Maggie, and I all felt this strange sense of anxiety when we were near the prop sword that Janice was holding when she collapsed. We think that was because the magic wasn't targeted at us specifically. It was more of a defense mechanism to deter other people from getting involved."

"Well, she's not having an anxiety attack now." Audrey's breath hitched. "She ... she collapsed. It didn't look like she was even br-breathing ..."

"Why don't we go to the hospital? I'm sure the doctors will be able to tell you more."

It would also give me a chance to keep talking to her and work my way to bringing up her mystery texting buddy. She nodded her agreement, and I downed the remnants of my tea before setting the cups in the sink to soak.

The hospital was only a few blocks away, but given the hour, it was safer to drive. Tania was busy tending to the rest of the guests, so I took the car keys from their hook by the front door and led the way outside. The ride over was awkwardly silent. I kept glancing at Audrey in the passenger seat, but it felt wrong to start accusing her of anything until we knew that Piper was going to be okay.

"Can I ask you something?" I broached as I pulled into a spot in the lot adjacent to the Emergency Room entrance at the hospital.

"Sure." Audrey's answer came out in a tired sigh.

"Is there a reason you tagged along for this tour? I mean, I get wanting to support Piper in her career, but it didn't look like you had much to do around the theater. Didn't it get boring?"

Audrey studied her hands in her lap. "I had Piper when I was pretty young. Not a teenage mother or anything, but I was still younger than a lot of my friends when they had children. I had wanted to be in theater. But that just didn't happen for me. I knew I'd have to give up certain things to be a mother."

"So, you got to sort of live out your dream by being on the tour."

"I just loved everything about it. The costumes, the lights, the set design. I helped a lot with that actually. But sometimes I think Piper would have preferred that I stayed home. She never said anything. But I got the sense she felt almost like I wasn't letting her grow up, because she had to take her mom with her."

"I'm sure she didn't feel that way," I insisted as I climbed out of the driver seat and into the early morning air. If anything, I suspected Piper felt stifled by her mum's refusal to talk about their magic rather than her presence in the theater. "Come on, let's go see how she's doing."

It wasn't hard to find Piper in the small Emergency Room. I spotted Benji in a partially curtained bay getting stitches to close the gash on his forehead. The way he kept moving to get away from the nurse suggested he had other things on his mind, or he didn't like needles. No doubt he, too, wanted to get an update on Piper's condition.

"I'm looking for information on my daughter, Piper Hennessey," Audrey told the charge nurse seated behind the central desk.

"Darcy, over here," Maggie's voice called. It drew me like a homing beacon, and I nudged Audrey over to stand in front of where my girlfriend sat in one of the hardbacked chairs along the wall. "They aren't sure what happened, but it looks like she's fighting some kind of infection," Maggie relayed.

"But she was fine an hour ago," Audrey protested.

"I think she came into contact with something magical and it's messing with her magic," I said in a hushed voice.

"Like what? The prop sword has been in evidence for days now," Maggie pointed out.

The knife.

"She touched a knife that Levi had been holding. It was only for a few seconds, but what if it was enough time for the magic imbued on it to mess with her?"

"How could it interfere with her magic?" Audrey asked, stepping closer to keep the conversation contained.

"Well, she's been struggling a bit with not letting her magic get built up. She sort of needed to let loose earlier. She got warm to the touch, even feverish and sweaty. Very much like what's happening now."

"It felt like my magic was turning on me," Maggie offered.

"You said it seemed like the sword turned Janice's real allergy on her even though there was nothing there, almost psychosomatic reaction," Audrey noted. "I hate to admit it, but Piper has battled some anxiety over the years, and I suspect I'm the cause. Could it be doing the same to her?"

"I think it's possible."

"Is it going to k-kill her?"

"I think knowing her mum is here with her, wanting her to fight, would do a world of good," I said. "Right, Maggie?"

"Yes. Just having you nearby might be enough to pull her out of whatever spiral the magic has her trapped in."

"I'll try anything."

"Let me go see if I can find the doctor who was working on her," Maggie said, standing and stretching before disappearing down a short hallway. That left Audrey and I standing alone in the middle of the Emergency Room.

"I did have to ask one other thing. Earlier, we accidentally found your phone," I began. "Piper said you've got the same phone case, so she mixes them up sometimes."

"They came as a two-pack," Audrey answered.

"Well, she sort of saw some texts with an unknown number and it sort of freaked her out. It looked like you were giving advice to someone dealing with some pretty intense romantic feelings—"

"I'm allowed to have private conversations," Audrey shot back.

"Yes, of course, it's just ... we think that Levi was getting help from someone within the production. I mean, he was able to slip by people by wearing costumes this last time. And everyone seemed to know he was harboring some pretty strong feelings for Janice ..." I couldn't bring myself to actually accuse this woman outright.

"And you think I let him in?"

"I don't ... I don't know."

"That young man was disturbed. He needed help, but not in a way I or anyone else around him could give."

She wasn't wrong there. The bloke definitely could have benefitted from psychiatric or therapeutic assessment. But that didn't explain who she was feeding romantic advice to via text. Or why she was so defensive about it.

"I know that Piper was feeling a lot of anxiety about the fact you were keeping this texting thing from her. Maybe if you could just explain what was going on, it might help her feel less anxious?"

I hoped wording it in terms of helping Piper heal would loosen Audrey's lips. Before she could say anything, Maggie returned with a slender dark-haired man in blue scrubs.

"You're Piper's mom?" he said, holding out a hand to Audrey.

"Yes. Please, tell me what's going on with my daughter."

The doctor glanced at me. "This is more of a private discussion."

"She's family," Audrey answered without looking at me.

"It seems that Piper is fighting some sort of unknown infection. She's not the first strange case we've had come through in the last couple of days."

"We know about Janice. They were in the same theater company," I offered.

"We're trying to push some broad spectrum antibiotics and other medication to try to bring her fever down. And we've got some cool blankets on her to try and bring down her temperature and keep her comfortable. But until we know more, that's all we can do." He held out a business card. "My name is Dr. Elijah Fitz. I'll be heading off shift soon, but I'm happy to keep in touch with any updates."

"Thank you." Audrey pocketed the card and followed Dr. Fitz to one of the far rooms where Piper lay hooked up to machines keeping track of her vitals. At least it appeared she didn't need help breathing.

Audrey sat at Piper's bedside and gave her daughter's hand a squeeze. "I'm sorry if any of this was my doing, sweetheart. I know I haven't always been the best communicator ... about a lot of things." She looked over at me. "I wasn't giving Levi Sanders romance tips. I was trying to help Benji get up the nerve to ask Piper on a date."

"Benji?"

"If you haven't noticed, he's a little socially awkward. But he seemed comfortable talking to me. And I thought he was sweet. A little nerdy, but he likes a lot of the same things Piper does."

"Did you ever notice anything strange happen around him?" I was beginning to get a sinking feeling in my gut.

"Strange? Not really, no."

"No sudden bouts of anxiety?" Maggie seemed to pick up on the same thing I had.

"I mean, we talked a little about our shared frustration that Piper only got to be Juliet's understudy."

"Why would Benji care?"

"We talked a lot about how I'd longed to be on stage and that I was so proud of Piper for even auditioning. I think he thought she deserved the role over Janice.”

She didn’t have to say whether he’d be willing to manipulate things in Piper’s favor. Pieces of the puzzle were starting to come into place, and I didn’t like the picture they were revealing. The inside man had been sitting right in front of us the whole time.

17

The realization of what she'd just revealed hit Audrey like a ton of bricks. She collapsed over Piper's prone body, shaking as she cried. There was still one piece of confirmation we needed. Audrey had been communicating in writing with Benji for months and was familiar with the way he wrote. The printed messages from Levi's camper flashed into my mind.

"Audrey, I think there's a way you can help put this all right," I said, saying a silent prayer that I'd brought my phone with me.

"How?" she asked through a hiccupping sob.

"You spent a lot of time writing to Benji. You probably became familiar with how he wrote. The types of words and phrases he used."

"I suppose so."

"Piper and I found some emails and other messages that Levi had from someone giving him inside information about the theaters on the tour and the troupe. It's probably how he knew not to stay at the B&B, even though it was closer to the theater and would put him closer to Janice," I explained, pulling up the images I'd taken during our impromptu visit to the camper.

I handed over the phone and allowed Audrey to scroll through the images, enlarging them as she pleased to study them. "It certainly sounds like him. But it isn't a username I'd seen him use before. But he used a lot of different ones for all the online games he played."

Maybe that's how he first came into contact with Levi in the first place? But it didn't matter. We had enough to link the pair of them together. Levi was already in custody, but that didn't mean we couldn't still use the plan Piper and I had concocted to catch Levi to get Benji to confess his involvement.

"Do you think Benji will go to the vigil tonight?" I asked.

"I mean, he doesn't like big social gatherings. Crowds are part of what he struggles with," Audrey answered. "But he'd try to go if it meant making Piper happy."

"And given that Piper has now landed herself in the hospital. People will know he was there, too. He might show up just to throw suspicion off himself," I noted.

"I really can't believe he'd be involved in something like this," she moaned.

"You're going to need to fill Rick and Vinnie in about what you've found and what you're planning," Maggie said to me.

"Already handled," I said, hoping Ginny would come through for me. Turning to Audrey I said, "Please call me if anything changes with Piper's condition."

"I will. And be careful. Whatever you're about to do, please don't put yourself in harm's way."

I couldn't make that promise to her. I had a feeling, however the rest of the day played out; I was going to end up right in the middle of potential harm. As Maggie and I left Piper's room and headed for the parking lot, I noticed that Benji had disappeared. That didn't bode well.

"What exactly is your plan?" Maggie asked once we were in the VW Bug.

"Ginny's planning to lend a hand at the vigil. She

said she'd pass along what we were planning to Chief Hayes."

"He won't be happy about that," Maggie noted.

"Yeah, but he'll have a murderer and an accomplice in custody when all is said and done."

"You know, I'm beginning to rethink my love of Shakespeare," Maggie said as I pulled to a stop outside her building.

"Don't let this nastiness sully your love for something," I told her. "It's already ruined two lives, probably three. Don't let it take that from you, too."

"It's just sad that people get so wrapped up in what they think is love that it ends in tragedy."

"Well, I can promise you that I won't be drinking poison or stabbing myself for you," I said with a smile.

"I'm going to hold you to that." She gave me a quick peck on the lips before climbing out. "You want to come up? It's bound to be quieter here than back at the B&B."

Quiet sounded perfect.

THE STRESS of the night's events had taken more out of me than I realized. When I woke again, it was almost noon. Maggie had laid out lunch for me and I greedily scarfed it down before grabbing a quick shower. I'd have to change when I got back to the B&B.

"You know, if you're going to be spending more time at my place, you should leave a few changes of clothes here, too," Maggie said from the doorway to the bathroom as I towel dried my hair.

"That feels like a big step," I admitted. "I'm not sure I'm quite ready for that yet."

"Well, the offer stands."

"Thank you for being the best girlfriend I could ask for."

"What are your plans for the rest of the day?"

"I was going to head back to the B&B to see what I can do to help Tania calm the mess that's been left behind and get everyone to the vigil. Hopefully, we'll be able to catch Benji and get him to admit to what he did."

"And if not?"

"Well, we've at least got enough evidence to convince Chief Hayes to bring him in for questioning."

"Go get 'em."

The B&B was in far better shape than I'd anticipated. The police tape was gone. Tania had already submitted the police report and charges were pending against Levi for the breaking and entering. She had taped off the broken window in the dining room and everyone appeared to be in relatively good spirits.

"How is Piper?" Tania asked after I'd changed my clothes to something more befitting a vigil.

"Hanging in there, I think. I'm not sure she was the intended target for what happened," I explained. "I think she just got hit by the side effects of the magic that Levi was slinging, and she had been in a heightened emotional state earlier in the night. It might have just messed with her head more than it had before."

"I didn't sense anything magical about him though," she noted.

"What do you mean? It's how he killed Janice. Didn't I tell you that?"

"It might be true that she was killed with magic. But that young man didn't do it."

"You can't know that for sure. Or ... Can you?"

"Over the years, I've learned to sense the difference between people with magic and those without. Those with magic tend to have stronger emotions, especially when they are using their abilities."

"And you didn't pick up on anything like that from Levi?"

"Not at all."

"But you weren't even in the same room as him. How could you really know?"

"I could feel his desperation and his sorrow. His grief was palpable. But he had no desire to harm anyone else. Only himself. And if he was using magic, I doubt he would need a weapon to achieve self-harm."

"So, you're saying what, Benji was the one with magic?"

"He was hard to read. Maybe that was intentional on his part. Or possibly he just never actively used his abilities while he was here. But if magic was indeed the reason Janice died, then it would have had to be him."

If he hadn't intended to use his magic, especially toward Piper, I could use that to push his buttons. It was a risky move, but I owed it to my cousin to get answers.

A little before five o'clock, the rest of the troupe with Tania and I headed back to the theater. I'd made a short trip over there earlier after getting changed to work a little of my own magic. I'd taken a few of the flowers we'd had growing around the house and encouraged them to replant themselves outside the theater. I'd gotten them to grow into the shape of Janice's name with a heart. It felt like the least I could do to honor the woman. And maybe I needed a little confidence boost before taking on Benji, too. Lucy and Celia set about organizing the rest of the troupe, ensuring everyone had candles with holders to avoid wax burns. Several towns-people arrived, as did strangers who shared that they'd come from neighboring towns where the show had passed through previously to pay their respects.

As the crowd grew, I scanned faces, hoping to spot Benji. There was every chance he'd bail on the gathering to go sit at Piper's side in the hospital. But that felt like something Audrey would warn me about. Especially as she was trying to assuage her own guilt in all of this. Finally, as Celia stepped up to the microphone to begin the vigil in earnest, I spotted him at the very back of the group. I picked up a candle and carried it around the perimeter of the throng. I caught Ginny's eye as I did and she mirrored my path, so we ended up on either side of Benji.

"How are you feeling?" I said, handing him the candle.

"Fine," he answered, accepting it without making eye contact.

"Have you seen Piper?"

"They wouldn't let me in to see her since I'm not family," he answered, a note of disgust in his voice.

"You know, I don't think you meant for her to get hurt."

That was enough to draw his attention. He turned his intense gaze on me. "What's that supposed to mean?"

"It means, I think you were hoping Levi would take himself out and you'd be able to support Piper while she stepped into the role you thought she deserved all along." There was no reason to pull punches now.

"You think you're so smart!" he shouted, drawing the attention of the assembled crowd, including Vinnie and Chief Hayes who stood off to one side.

"I think you were trying to impress her. You determined that getting her the chance to be in the spotlight instead of being the one directing was the way to do it. I'm not sure you meant to kill Janice either. I think you just wanted her out of the way, right?"

I watched as Ginny moved just a fraction of an inch closer. It was enough for her to place a hand on his wrist, making contact with the pulse point there. Benji's eyes went wide, and words tumbled out of his mouth.

"I didn't care if she died or not. She was pompous and stuck up. She thought everyone should worship the ground she walked on. Piper, she was the real talent. But no one was ever going to see that, not with Janice in the way."

"How'd you do it?" I pressed.

"I can do things ... make people's fears feel real. It's like magic. I knew she was terrified of peanuts. Threw a fit once when we walked past a candy store selling them. She wasn't anywhere near them, and she freaked out, like the whole world had to abide by what she needed."

"So, you put a spell on something you knew she'd have to touch," I prodded. "You wanted it to be a spectacle."

"It was easy. But those idiots in props were being overzealous and they broke it. I didn't mean for Piper to get mixed up in it."

"And did you reach out to Mr. Sanders?" Chief Hayes' voice entered the conversation.

"We met online. I knew he was obsessed with her. She was all he ever talked about. It made me sick. But I knew he would make the perfect fall guy.

So, I let him in the theater. I gave him the idea for the disguises. Anything to make it more plausible to get him to be there when she collapsed."

"You probably would have gotten away with it if you hadn't been texting Piper's mum about having feelings for her daughter," I pointed out. I conveniently didn't bother mentioning that Piper and I had discovered the messages between the two men in Levi's camper.

"Piper will forgive me. Everything I did was for her, to make her great. I've given her the chance to shine for everyone to see. Levi hated sharing Janice with anyone, but that's all I wanted for Piper. Her talent was wasted languishing behind the scenes. She deserved the spotlight. I love her!"

Ginny pulled her hand from his wrist as Chief Hayes and Vinnie closed ranks. There was no need for me to bind his hands in vines, even if I had the strong urge strong to punish this man for hurting my family. They took Benji away. I turned back to the vigil, making eye contact with Celia, hoping to convey my apology for interrupting. The smile and small head nod she offered in return appeared to acknowledge that she was grateful to be able to put all of this behind us.

"I want to thank everyone who came to help us

celebrate Janice. She was something special and we will miss her," Celia said, holding her candle aloft. "Let's give her one last standing ovation."

The assembled crowd erupted into cheers and applause at Celia's urging. I offered a small clap as Ginny settled in beside me. "You know, you aren't half bad at this whole detective thing. Maybe your talents are being wasted with Sage at High Time."

"Oh, no … I'm not a detective. I'll stick to growing plants."

"If you say so."

Just then, my phone buzzed with an incoming call from an unknown number. "Hello?"

"Darcy, it's Audrey."

"Is everything okay with Piper?"

"Yes. The fever's broken and she seems to be responding to the medication. They can't explain it, but they think she's going to make a full recovery."

Had Benji's arrest triggered something? Or maybe his confession? Could he have tried to see her earlier to fix what he'd done? "Benji is in custody. It's over."

"Thank God." There was static on the line for a moment and then she added, "I think I'm going to need to have a long talk with Piper when this is all over."

"I think she'd appreciate that. She loves you and wants to make you proud."

It was a sentiment I, too, struggled with when it came to my own parents. But I was starting to learn that sometimes the people whose love mattered the most weren't the ones we were born from. Sometimes love had to come from farther down the family tree.

18

The town gossip mill died down remarkably fast in the wake of Benji's arrest. I suspected Ginny had something to do with that, given she basically *was* the rumor mill in town. I still couldn't get the heartbroken look on Benji's face out of my head as Chief Hayes took him away. He really thought he'd had a chance with Piper.

Speaking of my cousin, I currently sat in the lobby of the hospital, waiting for her to be discharged as the clock ticked past six in the evening. It was still a marvel to me that even unconscious she'd been able to get a handle on her fire magic and keep that anxiety from doing her in. And maybe I hoped our connection had accounted for some of that strength.

Then again, maybe there was something to be said for our magic working in tandem. I'd used my magic with someone else before, but Doing it with family felt different. Stronger; almost like we had a sisterly bond . It was a feeling I wasn't going to forget any time soon. And one I already longed to find a way to repeat. I was building a community here in Brookhaven with Tania, Maggie, Beau, and Sam, but having Piper in the mix had filled a hole in my heart I never thought would mend.

After what felt like ages, the elevator dinged, and the doors parted to reveal Piper moving under her own power as Audrey fussed over her.

"I wish you hadn't told them you didn't need the wheelchair," Audrey said, trying to control the speed at which her daughter made a beeline for the exit.

"Mom, I can walk," Piper insisted, dismissing her mother's worries and waving her help off.

"Hey," I called to get my cousin's attention.

Piper halted her forward momentum and pivoted toward me. She offered a smile. "Hi, Darcy. You didn't have to come meet us. We can get back to the B&B ourselves."

"I know, but I wanted to be sure you were doing better."

"The doctors said I was lucky, but I've got a clean bill of health now."

"They wouldn't be releasing her otherwise," Audrey said, fiddling with her phone. "I'll get us a ride."

"Mom, it's literally two blocks away. I can walk."

With that declaration, Piper strode to the exit, leaving Audrey and I to trail behind her. I had to take a couple of large strides to reach Piper's side. "I'm honestly surprised you wanted to talk to me even after everything that just happened," I told her.

"Why? You didn't do anything," Piper answered.

"Well, I put you in danger almost immediately after we met."

She stopped walking. "I'm actually glad we went through this whole thing together."

"You are?"

"Yeah. If we could survive me nearly dying and being framed for murder on our very first family outing, we can get through anything."

We both burst out laughing. I bent over double, trying to catch my breath before I found words to speak. "It does seem to be something of a family trait. The getting accused of murder bit."

Piper cocked her head to the side. "Uh-huh, I'm going to need more than that."

"Oh, so after I moved here, there was this girl called Vera who was killed. Her body was left in the boot of Tania's car. I was driving it at the time, and I was the one who'd found her. So naturally, Chief Hayes thought I'd done it."

"You were innocent though, right?"

"Yes. Turned out she was running from her drug dealer boyfriend. She'd stolen some money from him. He caught up to her and killed her trying to find it."

"I don't feel so bad now," she replied with a smirk.

"Can I ask you something?" We approached the sidewalk leading up to Tania's B&B. There were far fewer vehicles than there'd been even a couple of days ago. Most of the troupe had moved on to the next town. I hadn't asked what would become of the Juliet role with the lead dead and the understudy convalescing in hospital.

"Ask away." Piper fiddled with the zipper on her jacket.

"Did you ever think Benji was behind it? I mean right after Janice's attack."

Piper hung her head. "Not at first. He acted as surprised as the rest of us. And he defended me when everyone else started saying I must have done it to get the part. We'd been friends for a while, but I never thought of him as anything more than that. He's not my type." Unshed tears sparkled in her eyes. "I feel like such an idiot for missing the signs for so long."

"People can be really good at hiding the darkness inside … and their feelings, too," I said. "Did you know he had magic?"

She shook her head. "It never even occurred to me. Though I guess looking back, there might have been a couple times he was using magic and I just wasn't aware."

"Or he ensured you didn't notice. It seems that people who can control other people's reactions and emotions are sometimes stronger than those of us with more elemental magic."

From behind us, I heard Audrey huffing and puffing as she powerwalked to catch up to us. I hadn't realized we'd been keeping such a quick pace. But as she hurried past us, I could see her cheeks were rosy from exertion and there were beads of sweat pooling on her upper lip. "I'm going to get our things, Piper and then we need to head out."

Piper and I sat on the front steps while Audrey went inside to gather their belongings. "Your mum must be happy that you get to be the lead actress in the play now."

"That's one of the things I was thinking about. I was happy being behind the scenes and I liked it. Being on stage, that was her dream. I think I let her push it on me, because I wanted to make her happy. And maybe Benji gave me a magical push along the way, too. For all I know he heard her talking about it so much that he orchestrated the whole thing."

"You can turn down the part, can't you?"

"We've only got a few more tour stops before we wrap. No one else has learned the lines and I know for a fact we've sold out shows up north. I don't really have a choice."

"Well, maybe once the tour is over, you and your mum can have a sit down talk and you can tell her how you really feel."

"I want to, but I'm scared of upsetting her. It's just been the two of us for so long. What if I lose her?"

"I know it's really hard not living up to what your parents expected of you. I don't think mine ever thought I'd be living in another country, doing plant magic. And I understand the fear of losing your mum more than you'd think. I'm pretty certain moving here cost me that relationship."

"At least you've gotten the chance to decide what you want to do with your life on your own terms."

"Stand up to her, then. Tell your mum that you're a grown woman and you can do what you want. You should be done living out her dream."

She offered a soft laugh. "I'm not sure I'm quite as brave as you."

I shook my head. "I think you missed the part where I literally ran to a different country an ocean apart to get away from my parents."

I sensed a presence behind me and turned to find Sam hovering halfway out of the front door. Piper craned her neck and gave a little start. "There's a guy ... uh, *in* the door."

"Yeah, that's Sam," I answered. "You're one of the first people to see him besides me and Tania. Well and Maggie."

"Did you just show up?" Piper addressed the ghost as he transitioned to be fully hovering on the porch.

"Oh, darling, I've been here for ages," he replied dramatically.

"I guess I didn't notice you before."

"I'm choosy about who I talk to," he said with a smirk. "And you were with so many boring mundane people it wasn't worth giving a headache to poor

Tania from having to deal with people claiming the place is haunted."

"But it is haunted," Piper pointed out flatly.

He waved off the comment and then added, "And since you're Darcy's family, that makes you someone I should know."

"I'm touched you care," I said with a laugh.

He offered me a wink and disappeared back into the house. Piper and I sat side by side on the front steps for a few moments longer in silence before the door opened behind us and Audrey appeared with their suitcases.

Piper stood and I followed suit. She pulled me into a fierce embrace. "Thank you for everything, cousin," she whispered in my ear.

"Message me when you get where you're going, so I know you both made it safely," I said.

"I promise."

I turned to Audrey. "It was nice to meet you, too."

"Thank you for saving Piper," she said, giving me a tentative hug.

"It's what family's for," I replied.

A cab pulled up in front of the B&B and Audrey led the way down the steps, setting the bags in the trunk. Piper offered one final wave before climbing in after her mother. I watched the cab pull away and turned to retreat inside when my phone rang with an incoming call. I looked to see Nan's number on the screen.

"Nan, it's late where you are, shouldn't you be in bed?" I answered.

"I was asleep when I woke up with the sudden urge to phone you," she replied. There was no trace of sleep in her tone. "You found Pauline's family?"

"Yes, I did. It's been quite the adventure."

"I could see it was going to be a bit rocky at first, but things have smoothed out I hope."

"Well, none of us landed in jail or turned up dead, so I'd say that's pretty smooth."

"I'm glad you've found people you can rely on that are close to you, love."

"Me, too." Silence fell on the line. I pulled the phone from my ear to check that the call was still connected. "Nan, you still there?"

"Yes, I'm still here. Just thinking about how far you've come in such a short amount of time. I'm so very proud of you, Darcy."

"You have no idea how much it means to hear you say that."

"I think we both know there's someone who you'd prefer to hear it from." The sadness in her voice tugged at my heart. She wasn't wrong. It would have meant even more coming from my mum and dad.

"Yeah, well, just because we've got magic doesn't mean we can perform miracles."

"Chin up, love. You're finding your place and I truly believe you are right where you're meant to be. If they come around to see how amazing you are, it will happen in its own time."

"I should let you get back to bed, Nan."

I ended the call and made my way inside, easing the front door shut behind me. I could hear Tania's voice coming from the kitchen. I found her mixing up what looked like cookie dough, with baking trays at the ready laid out on the counter.

"I would have thought after everything we'd just been through and everything you'd had to feel that you would want to take a break," I noted.

"Baking calms me," she answered and started spooning out dollops of dough onto the baking sheets. "And as you noted, after everything we've been through, I could use the stress relief."

"I will not argue with that."

In short order, Tania had doled out the contents of her mixing bowl and placed the cookies in the oven to bake. My mouth began to water as their aroma filled the kitchen. As Tania set about cleaning up the bowl and other utensils she'd used to make the dessert, I asked, "Are you sure you don't have hearth magic, too?"

"You've been waiting to ask me that for a long time now?" she replied.

"Well, there wasn't really a good time to bring it up."

"The answer is yes; I am certain I do not have that type of magic. It is simply a deeply instilled love of food I inherited from my Papa. As far as I am aware, I have never met anyone who had a gift for more than one type of magic."

"The more I learn about magic, the more I'm starting to realize it's as varied as the plants we've got growing here. Even among families, it can be so wildly different."

"It is certainly more complex than many of us believe when we first encounter it. But isn't that the beauty of it?"

"Yeah, it is," I agreed.

The scent of baking cookies filled the space and I leaned against my landlady's shoulder as we waited for the dessert to finish. The only thing that could have made this moment better was if Maggie were here. As if wishing made it so, a brief knock on the front door announced the entry of a visitor. A moment later, Maggie appeared.

Maybe I was wrong before and magic could perform miracles. I brightened at the sight of my girlfriend and folded myself into her embrace as she leaned in for a kiss. "Looks like this place is back to normal for a while anyway," she noted once our lips had parted.

"I am loathe to admit I could use the quiet for a few weeks," Tania said as the oven timer went off. She retrieved the baking sheets, setting them atop racks to cool.

My mouth watered at the sight of the cookies, and it took all my willpower not to snatch one before they were ready to eat. "It's going to sound horribly cliché, but I'm so glad I've got you both in my life," I announced.

"We count ourselves pretty lucky, too," Maggie said with a broad grin. "I mean, life was positively boring before you came along."

"She's not wrong," Sam's voice piped in from the front hallway.

"Like Tania said, I could use a little quiet for a while, too," I agreed.

In short order, Tania, Maggie, and I sat around the kitchen table, nibbling on cookies while another batch cooked in the oven. It was a lovely way to spend an afternoon. At this moment, everything was right in my world. Magic would no doubt bring new challenges for me to face, but I'd be ready.

QUICK AUTHOR'S NOTE

I WAS SO excited to expand Darcy's world a little and dig deeper into the magical lore of the world a bit. I had a blast creating the characters of her Nan and cousin Piper specifically. I wanted Darcy to know she had people who shared her blood that she could count on.

Like always, I knew I needed a good reason for Darcy to get wrapped up in the mystery and thus the idea was born that Piper was the lead's understudy and that would give her potential motive to take out the competition. Obviously I won't going to give our leading lady evil family so it meant I needed to figure out the actual killer. Initially there had been the plan for Benji to be the killer and behind the whole thing. But as I was writing, I came upon the idea of a stalker/super fan being involved and also becoming a scapegoat for Benji.

I also hadn't anticipated Benji having magic initially, but the more I worked on the plot, the more I liked that idea. And that he could turn fears against people. It all just fit really well.

I loved getting a chance to move Darcy and Maggie's relationship forward, since they are of course endgame. And as we move forward into the next few books, I am very excited to expand Darcy's connection to some other characters in town. It's about time she and Ginny get to have some fun together, too!

Turn the page for a sneak peek at what's next for Darcy...

Is blood thicker than magic?

Summer has come to Brookhaven and Darcy is soaking it up. Her magic is stronger than it's ever been and her relationship with Maggie is blossoming. They're even taking a weekend trip away as a couple!

But when she and Maggie stumble on a dead body with suspicious puncture marks in its neck and missing vital organs, she can't help but wonder just what other supernatural creatures lurk within the small town. Could things like vampires really exist?

As more bodies turn up, Darcy is determined to leave well enough alone. Until Tania goes missing and signs point to the same killer. Fearing that her mentor will become the next victim, Darcy races to find answers. Her search leads to the secretive inhabitants of Haven Island.

She'll have to rely on every bit of magical know-how to unearth the truth and save her friend's life.

Scan the QR code to buy High Harvest

ABOUT THE AUTHOR

S.E. Biglow is the pen name of *USA Today* bestselling author Sarah Biglow. She lives in Massachusetts with her husband and son. She is a licensed attorney and spends her days combatting employment discrimination as an Investigator with the Massachusetts Commission Against Discrimination.

You can find an up-to-date list of all my books here

www.ingramcontent.com/pod-product-compliance
Lightning Source LLC
Chambersburg PA
CBHW060815190726
48285CB00002B/679